THE

STURGEON'S

HEART

This is a work of fiction. Any resemblance to actual persons or events is coincidental.

Gibson House Press
Flossmoor, Illinois; Fort Collins, Colorado
GibsonHousePress.com

ISBNs: 978-1-948721-16-5 (paperback); 978-1-948721-17-2 (ebook)

LCCN: 2021938685

Cover and text design by Karen Sheets de Gracia
Text is set in the Adobe Caslon and Ambit typefaces.

THE

STURGEON'S

HEART

a novel

Amy E. Casey

CHICAGO · FORT COLLINS

For Scott

Something stirred in the fish. He was a monster of green gray, dragging his barbels along the bottom of the great stormy lake called Superior. Deep in his belly, he felt the river calling. The curling. The rustle of other slick bodies. The burst of life, the drive that spurred him up from the cold, calm lake bottom that was his deep and alien home. Because the river called, he would tilt up from the silt to thrash against current and fight up the mouth of the river to spawn. He had to go where the lake tapered to a point, pushing west toward bridges and lights. Where the shore gathered quietly, away from the surf that pounded against rock. Where it was shallow and safe.

While the fish made his decisions in his fish way, in his fish mind, the surface far above knew nothing about it. The lake remained its brilliant gray, even as sunlight beamed, starting to take the sky back from the springtime clouds. The towering conifers along the shore burrowed roots deeper into loam, one slow cell at a time. Ravens flapped from the jack pines like cloth caught in a gust. The air warmed, and the Minnesota spring slowly stretched itself awake. The red rock that eased into the water stood sentinel to the change, as it always had. The purple and black rock of the cliffs joined in listening. And far below, urgency slammed hard at the fish's consciousness. Go, he thought. Go.

Need pulsed within, and the fish and all his brothers headed west.

Part One

1

HOWARD WRIGHT WAS ALWAYS COLD, even during the fleeting Duluth summers. Part of it was the chill of the night wind that came in through his upstairs apartment window, bearing with it news of the lake's ever-shifting mood. But part of it was just him. Sitting in the dark, tapping away at the keys of his laptop, he nestled his chin further down into the collar of his gray turtleneck. Wearing it always made him feel like more of a real writer than he was. Technical writing one-off gigs and a regular stream of reviews and articles helped him get by well enough, even if he was just a hack. But he did his best. He wrote constantly, obsessively. Sticky notes and pages filled with scrawl made neat piles in every room, on his worn leather armchair, on the kitchen counter, beside the bed. He tried not to cash the checks his mother sent along in the mail, but most months he had to. He supposed she had a right to buy a few words from him a few times a year. But he was here, making it, more or less, at age thirty-three. He was grateful to be away from her. Away from everyone. Howard rarely talked to anybody. It was easiest that way. Less irrational pain in the belly. More time happily locked away inside the apartment. There were loose baseboards in most of the rooms, and the kitchen faucet dripped incessantly, but he hadn't gotten around to fixing them. He liked the apartment just fine the way it was, brown and small.

Shivering, Howard lifted a blanket from its peg on the wall next to the desk and wrapped it around his shoulders. He eyed the window across the room—served him right for opening it in the first place. Even in the weak light from the laptop, he noticed his hands looking dark with cold, almost purple as he struck the keys. Still, he kept typing. The article was about the changing face of transit amid the rise of ridesharing apps. He found the topic engaging, and he had a fondness for the publication that requested it. They had been encouraging about his work in the past and kept asking him for more submissions. Howard liked feeling sure of things. It felt good to click "submit." Another small check toward the rent.

He ran a hand through his almond hair and opened his email, remembering a notification that he'd ignored earlier. There was a message from a woman interested in buying his truck. So, someone had already seen the For Sale sign. If he was honest with himself, Howard was still reluctant to let go of the old 2001 pickup. Now that he'd started getting his groceries delivered, he rarely drove anywhere, and he thought he might be able to get two grand for it. But he still wasn't sure. He marked the message as unread. He'd deal with that later. He blew hot air into his cupped hands. Why was it still so damn cold in the middle of May? He stood up to shut the window and saw gray spots floating in front of his eyes in the dark. Maybe he was coming down with something. A glance at the clock. Late. He draped the blanket back on its peg. He pushed his fists into his lower back, stretched, and shuffled into the bathroom to brush his teeth. He flipped on the light.

The mirror confronted him with the beginning of how everything changed. Howard's childhood imaginings of what walked in the dark woods at the back of his parents' property, the bloody ghosts of his dreams, they arrived, right there in the glass. They had caught up with him after all.

Struck, Howard tore his turtleneck over his head and slid his arms out of the sleeves. The shirt fell from his hands to the floor.

He couldn't rasp the air in fast enough. The mirror.

He ran his hands over his thin chest. A high, piercing whine seemed to envelop his head as he gaped at what absolutely couldn't be real: a being of translucent flesh, with slick, red blood shining through everywhere underneath. Deep blue stripes—his veins, prominently visible—branched across his arms and chest. Bringing his face close to the mirror, Howard could see them arching out, even from his filmy eyelids. Through the red cheek muscle, he saw the faint outlines of his molars. The darkish trees, these fractals of capillaries against a canvas of red muscle fibers, netted his skin. All was monstrous red.

Howard tried to make a sound, to scream. The high whine grew louder, and then—darkness and falling. Past the floor and into a deep and hollow burrow of nothing. He dreamt, then, of pinpoints of distant light, a constellation moving. It was doubled into parallel image below, across a windless, black mantle of ice. Inky sweetness overcame him, and he gave himself over to it entirely.

His body, lying still on the bathroom floor, grew colder and more alive than ever. If anyone else had been there, they might have heard the flesh hum. The crumpled monster slept. Unfortunately for the remarkable body, it still had the heart of a quiet, frightened man.

2

ON THAT SAME EVENING, four streets further away from the lake, Sarah Turnsfield was one hour into her cashiering shift at Ahlborn's, the 24-hour natural food co-op that operated on the edge of downtown Duluth. The compact, russet brick building was at the top of a steep road and, like so many others in the city, built into the hills that lined Superior's shore. At night, all the lights from the buildings and streetlamps were visible for miles from Canal Park at the bottom. From there, anyone could look up into the city of staggered topography, allowing room enough for it all to illuminate, up and up and up, flashing in or out as businesses closed, people went to sleep. But the lights at Ahlborn's were always on.

Sarah preferred to work the mostly dead hours of the night at the store, which were barely staffed and sparely attended. The co-op members were adamant about keeping the round-the-clock hours, though, and just enough wandering seekers of supplements or improbable carts full of midnight organic groceries slid in and out of the doors each night to justify the presence of a manager and at least one cashier. The way people drifted into the store in the middle of the night, often alone, felt like its own kind of meditation. Sarah left them uninterrupted. She rarely spoke unless someone asked her a question.

Brown cardboard displays with handwritten signs showcased the newest items, and a spread of local sweets and nuts stretched along one side wall, waiting to be scooped from their clear containers and dropped into cellophane bags. An array of herbal remedies dominated a corner of the store. The pastries, brought over from the bakery down the street, were dense and stickily glazed, and the produce section, piled high with fruits and vegetables along the front aisle, smelled cold and citrusy. The lights buzzed. Greenish outdoor carpeting surrounded the cart corral. Ahlborn's was an institution to those who loved it. It had a whimsy and doubt about it all at once, like the belief that anything can be cured by drinking the right kind of tea.

Ahlborn's employees—like Sarah—were often eccentric, but they were appreciated by the clientele for their knowledge of the store and the properties of its foodstuffs. During the growing season, the store even ran its own vegetable garden, which took up two acres just a few miles north. Scaring wildlife away from the plants and keeping things watered was a perennially popular summer job for the teenagers lucky enough to be hired by Frank, the ageless, skinny owner with blond dreadlocks who had been running the store since anyone could remember. Most people loved Frank. Sarah was, as she was toward everyone, indifferent.

In the stretches of inactivity between customers, Sarah bit her lip compulsively and flicked her eyes from side to side, keeping watch over everything under the fluorescent lights that blazed from their straight rows on the ceiling. People often remarked that Sarah looked much younger than her fifty years. She was slim and beautiful, with a memorable face, which she usually hid behind shining twin curtains of straight, gray-blond hair.

It was a slow evening. Bending her chin down, Sarah stared at the conveyor belt until she heard the entrance door slide open. A young woman in a bright green sweater entered the store and shot a brief, close-lipped smile at Sarah before walking briskly toward the produce section. She gathered an armful of strawberry cartons and then headed over to the freezers. She soon returned and spilled the jumble of packaged fruit and a small container of frozen yogurt down at Sarah's register. With a quick apology, and checking to see that no other customers were standing in line behind her, she took off to the back of the store toward the liquor section. She jogged back to the register with two bottles of Jack Daniel's, which she added to the belt. She smiled at Sarah, a flush burning across her pale cheeks. "How are you tonight?" she asked, curling her short black hair behind her ear. The older woman paused, disconnected and expressionless. She was looking at the berries.

"Strawberries," Sarah finally said, eyes and mouth pointed toward the fruit itself rather than the customer in front of her. "Strawberries are close genetic relatives to roses. It's interesting, isn't it? They don't look like them at all." The young woman opened her mouth, then closed it again.

Sarah scanned the fruit, the frozen yogurt, and stopped at the bottles. "Can't do these," she said. "After 10 p.m. No alcohol."

"Shit. Are you sure?" the young woman said. The flush across her cheeks deepened.

"Sorry." Their eyes met briefly before Sarah's dropped back down.

"Well, I guess I can make it until tomorrow," the customer said, adding a laugh at the end. Sarah just stared.

"Fifteen dollars and eighty-five cents."

The young woman handed over two tens. Sarah made the change, pressing each bill and coin one at a time into her open palm as the whiskey bottles stood listlessly at the end of the conveyor belt. In the minute that followed, the two of them worked silently together to load the items into one paper bag. The customer then thanked Sarah, to no response, and walked out into the night.

3

JO EXITED THROUGH THE SLIDING doors of Ahlborn's and shifted the grocery bag to a more comfortable place against her hip. She stepped along the sidewalk in the dark, thinking about how sometimes, and now more than ever, she still felt that she looked like a girl. Her chest was flat, and she barely topped five feet in heels. It was why she cropped her dark hair so short—she felt she looked more polished. A short cut had a style to it. College girls always had that long, shiny hair. Jo did not. She was twenty-eight, she was past all that. She had already landed her first adult job in marketing. Granted, it was small-time. Granted, it was only because someone who knew her folks back home in Colesburg found her a way in. Granted, she had just quit.

Leaving Iowa for Duluth was easier than she thought it would be. The two weeks after her resignation notice passed quickly, and the way her colleagues drifted silently around her made it seem like she had already gone. So much the better, she thought. The following weekend, she paid a driver to get her to the Greyhound station in Cedar Rapids and made her way north to this city, with four tote bags, a cat carrier, and a rolling suitcase. As the first hour of that bus ride clicked by, she'd felt something close to sleep. Pulling north, out of Iowa, loosened the tightness in her throat. The window rattled against her pressed cheek. She tried not to think about leaving her old bedroom for the last time, how she had clutched at the dresser knobs as she sank to the floor, the sobs cracking out of her. It was all so pathetic. Her eyes hurt. It was time to go—she had known it for a while. Her college roommate had always sung the praises of Duluth. It was as good a place as anywhere, she thought. It was far away. And now, here she was, walking home, or whatever that meant now, through the night.

This would be her city now. She wanted something new and as different from Colesburg as possible. Somewhere less flat, less green, with more to offer than fundraising banquets at the small white churches that looked like houses, where all the neighbors were people who had known her since she was holding her mother's hand in white tights and buckled shoes. Where everywhere she looked was a street she had walked down with someone she'd loved or known once. She could almost taste her own shadow, lean like her high school self. An antic, attached to her psyche, recursively striding down the winding park path during the golden hours of sunset, laughing about things that she couldn't remember anymore.

The north-moving bus had outrun that shadow. Duluth had a different kind of sunlight. The lease on Jo's new apartment was freshly signed, and she had already negotiated her way into a temporary summer job at Trenton Floral and Design, a little downtown flower shop within walking distance from her new place. She had that job, plus her savings. The apartment came furnished with an old bed and couch, and she scouted garage sales for the rest of what she needed. Her things were still in her bags, but the space was slowly coming together. She was doing fine.

Not far from her apartment, the city skyline was dominated by the imposing, wondrous lake. The same gray watery planes echoed in the industrial landscape. Jo loved the tall matte rectangles of the buildings—they spoke to an era of rising concrete, machinery, and enterprise. The enterprises that drove the city were different now, but the layers of steel and glass still stood against the rising hills with a worn, respectable grace. And there was youth, too, playing against the backdrop. A vibrant waterfront peppered with restaurants, shops, gardens, and walkways spoke to the forward-facing city, with its eyes toward the shoreline and out beyond. Steamers drifted into the large northern port. From a distance, they seemed to move on the water like ghosts. Some of them still carried iron ore, or coal, or grain, after fifty years of service, steadily cutting through the fresh water of the inland sea as they had done for decades. The grid of the city was, in some ways, much like an extension of those shipping routes: trajectories washed in by the waves and calcified upon the hills.

So far, Jo found the people in Duluth to be courteous and giving but sparing of true warmth as a rule. It was that northern keep-to-oneself sensibility, and Jo found it fresh. There were few unprompted questions here. This life was one where she could find her way without anyone particularly noticing. Duluth offered itself to anyone ready to create their own world within its rugged boundaries, but only if that world could stand against a stark chill for nine months out of the year. The walk to work would be a frigid one in winter, but Jo didn't need to worry about that now. She needed to focus on what was immediate. The weather was steady and warming now, with spring hitting its late bloom. She hoped to eventually buy the truck she'd seen in the parking lot behind her apartment building: a green Ford pickup with a For Sale sign in the back cab window. She'd emailed the seller—no response yet. But there was plenty of time. Right now, the only thing she needed to do was carry her groceries safely home through the night.

Jo sighed. The paper grocery bag crunched, held tight in her arms, and her black flats made an echoing flap against the sidewalk as she walked. She stopped at the street corner, a little confused, and almost turned down the wrong street. Everything was still new enough to look the same in the dark. She passed a woman in black athletic wear walking a German shepherd. The nighttime traffic noise and wind both started to sound louder than Jo remembered. Crossing over to the right side of the street, Jo told herself to be sensible, to remember that everything would be fine. A car alarm triggered in the distance, and she scuffed her ankle against the curb, stumbling. Where was her apartment building? Did she pass it already? The frozen yogurt burned cold on her bare arms through the paper grocery bag. Then, her eyes homed in on the sight of the building, another block down, the same sight she'd started recognizing. It was just different in the dark, thought Jo, chiding herself. She needed to stop worrying so much.

Jo waved her fob at the building entrance and passed brass mailboxes before climbing the thin stairwell leading up to her floor. As she fumbled for the keys to unit 15, she could feel her blood starting to stir at the hollow sounds surrounding her, at the odd smell of the carpeting. Her keys weren't in her right pocket as she'd thought. Was that someone else coming up the stairs? She shifted the grocery bag to her other hip. Something inside her fluttered. She didn't really know how safe she was. How easy would it be for anyone to come up behind her, to grab her by the wrists? She coached herself out of the terrible thought. If only she could just open the damn door. Jo crammed her hand hard into the left pocket of her jeans, finally drawing her keys out, only to drop them in front of the door. She bent down, snatched them up. She tried the key in the lock and swore when it wouldn't turn. Her fingers wouldn't cooperate. Was it the silver key instead? Jo heard her cat Ike mewing on the other side of the door, and noticed her pulse rise as she made another botched attempt with the wrong key. "I'm coming, little guy," she whispered into the door, and slipped the correct key in. Finally, the lock flipped.

She slid in the door, turning sideways to keep Ike from dashing out. Setting the bag and keys on the table, she cracked a smile, laughed weakly, and scooped up the noisy gray cat. "Hey, love," she said. She buried her face in his fur and squeezed a small meow out of him. Before she could finish telling him "I'm home," her voice cracked. She tried to stop the shudder of tears.

Every sob she half-stifled echoed against the angles of the room. The lamp she'd left on for Ike looked spare and friendless standing in the middle of the floor. The couch slumped beneath the ragtag secondhand quilt she'd bought to cover the stain on the side. The yellow lamplight intensified the little scars and unevenness of the blank walls where holes for hanging pictures had been made and filled back up again. Her bags that she'd taken on the bus were still by the door, still filled to bursting, sleeves of shirts spilling out where she'd crammed them back in. The sticky silhouette of a removed butterfly sticker was visible on the side of the refrigerator. It was still only the idea of a home. She put a hand to the kitchen counter to steady herself.

Several pieces of frost on the surface of the frozen yogurt container pooled into a puddle before she remembered to place it safely in her freezer. It took longer still for her to move from the kitchen to the bedroom and turn off the lamp. She climbed into the left side of the bed, nose still feeling puffy and full, laying herself neatly parallel to the edge. Jo inevitably drifted to the middle of the saggy mattress in sleep, her knees clutched tight up to her chest and one arm outstretched toward the empty pillow she still kept on the other side.

4

WHEN JO'S SEVEN O'CLOCK ALARM went off, the sun was already casting through her yellowed bedroom blinds. She propped both pillows up against the headboard and blinked groggily at the walls around her. She felt a sense of newness and immediacy. It was morning. She was in control of these rooms, small as they were. Just her. She thought about finding some art for the walls. They looked so blank.

She flipped on the song she was loving lately, by the female vocalist with the flutelike voice, and started the tub running. Once lowered in, she made shapes of her short hair as she ran the shampoo through. She looked down over her submerged self, that dark shock of hair, that wiry body, the shimmer of stretch marks that asserted themselves years ago but seemed more prominent now. She placed her hands over her tiny breasts. Everything was a game now. She didn't believe that anyone would glance her way, not without her efforts to fool them into it at least, but maybe if she tried. She couldn't help her longing for someone else's hands. She only owned bright colors. She was fun, wasn't she? It wasn't so bad. Her mouth was a nice shape, she knew it was.

She dried off quickly.

A streak of red lipstick, a scratch of the cat's ear, and she was down the stairs and off to her first day at Trenton Floral. Walking up the sidewalk, she admired the look of the morning light on the city. The fragile feelings that overwhelmed her last night now seemed ridiculous. Everything was crisp and moving—cars and bicycles zipped by on the street. She passed other apartment buildings, much like hers, made of worn brick with the occasional window boarded up. There were big old Victorian houses, three-story affairs, some lots with trellised gardens and others crowded with tall weeds. But all of it was blessed by the lake air and felt right to her. With each step, Jo felt a greater conviction pulling her forward. She practiced glancing straight into the eyes of each person she passed, smiling winsomely, open, instead of looking down. Four blocks away from the lake and two to the left, she arrived at work.

As Jo stepped into Trenton Floral, two smiles met her immediately—one from an old, impish woman named Ruth, and another from the immaculately manicured lead designer, Tonya, who Jo remembered from her interview. Tonya's long braids swayed as she walked forward and stretched out her hand to shake Jo's. "Welcome, Jo. It's great to see you again. Thanks for coming in to start with us right away."

Jo beamed. "Hey, thanks, I'm happy to be here. I'm so glad you needed the help." For half a second, she considered qualifying that statement further, but decided against it. They had seen her resume. They knew what her previous job had been. There was no real reason to bring up how odd it felt to be somewhere so different from the cubicle she'd practically lived in, the ever-growing list of client accounts, and the pressure of constant internal and external opinions that made her question her own taste. Shedding all that was worth the pay cut, at least for now. After feeling so stuck for so long, the words *seasonal* and *temporary* tasted like cool summer lemonade in her mouth.

Tonya's warm voice brought Jo back to the moment, back to the displays overflowing with gardenias and hibiscus, back to the glowing cooler with vases of cut flowers in every hue. The large display windows at the front of the store created a frame around the moving picture of the passersby on the city street, and small metallic ornaments throughout the store reflected points of light from the chandeliers overhead. It was almost difficult to believe in the teeming space that unfolded inside the shop, which looked so small and tired in its aging vinyl siding from the outside. But inside, it was a near-wonderland overflowing with green. Tillandsia hung in glass orbs at staggered heights, and huge green-and-purple-leaved spiderwort planters swung from the wooden rafters that ran across the ceiling. Philodendrons sprawled in large blue pots in the corners, stretching their thick stems and shiny leaves upward. Long counters further into the shop allowed designers to process plants and create arrangements for waiting customers, who inevitably looked upward and breathed in deeply while they waited, safely cocooned by the dark walls that seemed an understory of profound depth. Rows of leafy shadows intensified the illusion. The air was humid and lush, smelling always of newly unwrapped blossoms and leaves. Buckets packed with flaring petals sat in rows, and a stunning white orchid sprouted from its pot on a corner shelf. It was a good place.

"We've got plenty of design work for you, I promise," said Tonya. "Ruth can show you what we're working on right now. Corsages and boutonnieres, then we're on to the table arrangements. Big wedding this weekend. You let me know if you need anything. I've got paperwork to take care of, but from what you sent along in your email last week, you know what you're doing, Jo. I'll be back to check on you in a while." Tonya slipped into the back office. Jo's smile shook as the compliment swam in her brain.

"Come on over here, honey!" said Ruth, waving Jo toward her workspace. Ruth had a halo of hair as white as confectioners' sugar, and a lilac fragrance about her. Even as she beckoned Jo, Ruth's fingers kept expertly twisting ribbon into tiny bows, the perfection of decades of practice. Amid the muted trumpet sounds of an old Miles Davis album gliding through the shop and the intermittent clanging of the telephone ring, they worked side by side. Jo felt instantly at home, remembering her years of earning money for college each summer back in Iowa, working at the flower shop owned by her mother's best friend. The work was familiar and enjoyable. What Jo didn't instinctively remember, Ruth smartly guided her through, her cool hands over Jo's own.

They had lunch together with Tonya, gulping down bites of turkey sandwiches in between getting up to wrap bouquets for customers who rang the service bell at the counter. They checked tasks off the list with neat precision. Before Jo could even wonder if six o'clock had come, it had. Ruth was out the door first. She grabbed her bag, waved a chipper "See you ladies!" and ran off, no doubt going home to the retired husband and ten-year-old basset hound she had told Jo so much about. Tonya locked the back doors, and Jo made circles of leaves into piles as she swept the floor behind the counter. The sweep of the broom felt satisfying as more and more of the floor was cleared away. She scooped the waxy green mounds into the dustpan one by one. Jo watched Tonya work through the closing tasks. Her dark, lustrous arms were tense with grace. Tonya moved so easily in her body that Jo felt the awkward jumble of her own limbs even more keenly.

"Thanks for showing me around today," Jo said, "You have no idea what this job means to me. I'm looking forward to my time here." She realized that she sounded rehearsed and trite, but she hoped that her face would show the truth, that she was sincere.

"You know what—you did a wonderful job today. I'm so glad to have you on board, Jo." Tonya's gold bracelets jangled as she put a few last items back in the cabinet. "You heading out now?"

"Yeah," Jo said, "Think I'm going to catch dinner at that place just on the corner—there's a little café on the lower level. My friend Cait owns it. Hoping to see her there. We went to school together at U of M."

"Really? They do have great soup. The chicken and wild rice, especially. One of the best I've had." Tonya started flipping the light switches inside the cooler cases one by one, each going dark with a pleasing click.

"See you," said Jo, nodding. She took her purse and walked out into the early evening with a hot cup of soup and a hot cup of coffee on her mind. She thought she might take both to go, though—bring them back to the apartment and see the cat. The dingy little place still didn't feel quite like home, but if she spent more time there, she thought it might click together. The day at Trenton had warmed her through, and she hoped that warmth would stay, rather than dissipating out from her like it had last night. She could get that carton of soup and give Ike some, on his new favorite perch on the radiator. She could clean up the glasses around the sink and unpack some more things from her bags. She could get her shoulders warm. She could try feeling at home.

5

HOWARD AWOKE ON THE bathroom floor. He saw the worn spots where he'd scuffed the white paint on the cabinet under the sink. Sun flooded in from the window.

He lifted his arm and saw blood-red daylight shining straight through the thinner skin between the fingers of his upheld hand.

Horrified, he scuttled forward and up on to his bed in the next room, huddling there in a crouch with blankets pulled tight around him. Panic shot through his body. He struggled to breathe. He hid his reticulated hands from himself within the blankets. He cracked the back of his head against the wall. Pain exploded at the base of his skull. He willed himself to inhale. *Breathe, goddammit.* It was real. Somehow. All real. He was a transparent man. A monstrous pile of visible blood and gristle. He was trapped in this terrifying body. The familiar room around him seemed entirely dissonant to this new reality. He grasped for comprehension.

Howard calmed his breathing by focusing on an object. On the shelf on the wall facing the bed, he had a ship in a bottle—his favorite one, one that he had made himself. The bottle's glass was thick and shining, distorting the model ship just enough to imbue it with a sense of movement. Howard inhaled—*one, two, three, four.* To fit the thin pieces of wood just so, through the neck of the bottle and atop the waiting glue, was an art. He exhaled—*one, two, three, four.* The sails were made of paper. Toothpick masts were inserted while collapsed, then raised inside the bottle from delicate threads attached and smoothly pulled from the outside. Howard looked at his hand again. Roiling waves of red moved beneath the skin. A world within a world. His vision faded in and out. He glanced toward the pile of books on the shelf next to the ship—old editions of Asimov and Bradbury, covers in muted tones. He breathed. He kept the shelf as his horizon, the bed as a raft being pitched by the waves.

He willed himself to think through things logically, one step at a time. He had no medical coverage, to start with. He didn't go to hospitals. The last time he'd been in a doctor's office was when he was twelve years old. The thought of dry, gloved hands and expensive brown shoes worn at the tip brought the taste of bile to his throat. It wasn't the fault of the doctor he saw that last time. The man's eyes could cripple with their sincerity. Howard remembered how much he'd hated himself for wanting, so badly, to dive into the kindness of those eyes, instead of hearing the words that the man was saying. He remembered the white surgical mask tugged down beneath the man's chin. It wasn't the doctor's fault, of course; no one wants the job of telling twelve-year-old boys that their fathers won't wake up again, that the roads were slick, and it could have happened to anyone. He could still smell the latex. He still couldn't set foot inside a clinic. Everything about medical facilities repulsed him.

Instead, Howard typically took to the internet. Searching his book-marked medical resource sites and forum threads, he felt confident enough to sensibly diagnose himself. One time, with a persistent sinus infection, he saw an online physician over video chat to get an antibiotic prescribed. He remembered turning away so that man wouldn't see his distress. It had taken him another day to work up the nerve to pick up the prescription at the pharmacy. He took the pills out right away, pouring them into a bowl so he didn't have to look at the wretched orange container, the doctor's name in type. But he had done it. Followed through, took the pills, and gotten better. He could do that again. He still had the login for the site, he was sure of it. The idea of the money was something to deal with later. He had to do something.

He needed to take control. Rising from the bed, he resisted any urge to wash or urinate—the thought of facing the mirror again was like a contaminated needle. He let the blankets fall away from his shoulders. His forearms, glassier and more crimson than ever in the morning glow, revolted him. He snatched a long-sleeved shirt from the dresser and tugged it on. He found the laptop, innocently sitting where he had left it last night. He opened it and started to type into the search engine. His hands seared bright red as they rested on the keys, and his heart sang of fear. He needed to focus. He wanted to rehearse what he would say in his head, but he could think of nothing. He found the service he'd used in the past and frantically began filling out his information for an online appointment.

The cursor clipped down the screen, but it got stalled blinking against the white field that asked him to describe the reason for his appointment. What on earth could he write? He imagined closing the computer and walking away. He imagined the hood of a black jacket shielding his face, he saw himself tearing away down the road in the truck, driving away as far as he could get on the back roads. Getting lost somewhere near the Canadian border. Alone. But what would he do then? His hips numbed in a wave of warmth. His neck twinged. He would still have this body.

That thought jarred him. He stood up.

Howard started to pace a scribbled path around his apartment. He opened the kitchen cabinet where he kept vitamins and supplements. Prepared for all inevitabilities, classified and organized. He looked at the lists of everyday procedures and processes he had taped up on the outside of the cabinet. It all seemed incredibly small and stupid now. He was awash with the same feeling he'd constantly fought himself out of as a teenager, agoraphobic and paralyzed. Back then, he'd developed a debilitating resistance to going outside, for seeing strangers without a clear sightline to their faces. He'd worked up this theory that a strange man would come around a corner someday, emerging out of shadow with his father's face. He used to fixate on that idea of seeing his father again, and of being unprepared. In Howard's mind, he would meet his father's eyes, only to witness him disintegrating—pouring in a dry cascade out of a pant leg and blowing away like sand, the eyes last. That thought slipped back in so easily. He'd lived alongside it for so many years that it was embedded in his adolescent psyche, a daily inevitability. In that time of his life, he was used to being a child who saw things, and he used the strategies his therapist had taught him to overcome it as he had the others.

But now, those banished visions of Howard's youth seemed to place themselves beside his reality at a new angle, disorienting him. The truth fought toward the surface as it had ten thousand times. His father, he reminded himself, had died in a hospital bed two decades ago, after an icy and chaotic burst, his car flying down a country road in the reckless confidence of having known those snowy roads all his life. God forgive him.

Howard forgot where he was. He was standing in snow, looking up at the stars, vibrant in the dark against the black velvet sky.

No, no, he was in the kitchen. He was ill. He felt so cold. His hands shook.

He staggered to the chair, picked up the laptop again. He couldn't avoid this. He told himself to just fill out the damn medical form. His stomach clenched, but he finished it. He entered the online queue for an appointment. The doctor would sign on to see him in seven minutes.

He had no idea what to say—he checked "no" next to almost every symptom description on the intake form. He was sure the doctor wouldn't be prepared for what he was about to see. Howard set the laptop on a chair and sat down on the floor. Just his knee appeared in the video frame. He tilted the screen up. He knew the resolution of his webcam was low. He tried scooting back several feet. There. He could see the blur of himself, but it looked small and shadowed in the frame, his red face cast into gray. He would have to speak loudly for the microphone to pick him up, but his face and the truth of his body would stay distorted. Good.

A countdown began on the screen. "Your doctor is entering the room" lit up in white text against a blue box. Howard slid back another half of a foot. He knew it looked insane.

When the doctor signed on, he appeared in a white coat. He had a dark mustache and a clipboard. He greeted Howard.

"Hello, Mr. Wright? Howard? I'm Doctor Groshek. I'm having some trouble seeing you—are you able to come closer to the screen?"

"I need to stay over here, trust me," said Howard, too loud, forcing the words over the tightness in his voice.

The doctor cleared his throat. "It will be easier for us to conduct the appointment if you come closer, but as long as you can speak up from over there, let's just start with a couple questions. It says in your form that you are experiencing some redness or irritation on your skin. Is that correct?"

"Well," said Howard, and stopped there. He breathed in deeply. The doctor waited. From where he was, Howard couldn't tell if the man was looking at him or looking down.

"Could you tell me where you're experiencing the irritation?" he asked. Howard noticed him tap his pen against his clipboard while he waited for an answer.

"It's everywhere," said Howard. "But it's not . . . it's different. I'm sorry, I'm not . . . I don't think I'm well at all. I've been having a hard time with this."

"If you don't mind coming closer to the screen and showing me, say, your arm, we can take a look. Otherwise, I might not be able to help you today. If I can't see the problem, I can't diagnose anything, unfortunately. I'm really having trouble seeing you from where you are."

Howard put a fist to his lips and looked helplessly at the screen. His jaw was shaking. "Please," he said, "I'm disappearing." The doctor looked unsettled. "I can see through my own skin. There's no color to me—it's as if my skin is made of glass. And the blood beneath. Jesus, look at me!"

The doctor squinted closely at his screen. Howard crawled up closer, hand and knee and hand, until he confronted the screen. He pushed his sleeve up and held his arm out to the webcam. The networks of veins and sinew flicked like red robotics beneath his wrist as Howard clenched and unclenched his hand. The full roundness of his eyeballs sat within the clear, blood-filled casing of his face. The doctor could see the constant stare—though blurred—even as Howard's pale eyelids closed and trembled in supplication. The doctor's lips began the word *what?* He looked shaken, then immediately angry. He said nothing. The screen went blank.

A new message appeared in cheerful blue text: "Your appointment is finished. Check your account email for important follow-up information from your doctor." The veins in Howard's forehead and temples darkened as his neck muscles pulled taut.

He was alone. Vibrations rippled across his skin. He swore he saw snow start to fall.

6

SARAH SPUN THE WIDE OLD steering wheel of her Cutlass station wagon to the left, turning into her usual spot in the last row of Ahlborn's parking lot, ready to start her shift. The small lot, normally somewhere between scattered and packed, was oddly vacant. She walked up to the employee entrance, noticing that it looked dark inside. She saw some orange cones off to the side of the building as well. She guessed that she'd missed a voicemail, which wasn't unusual. Her prepaid cell phone didn't always forward messages correctly, or record calls for that matter. She nearly never checked it anyway.

She saw the sign taped to the entrance soon enough, written on cardboard with permanent marker. Frank's haphazard scrawl explained that a water main had burst out front, and Ahlborn's was closed until the next afternoon for cleanup of some minor flooding issues. Sarah resented the waste of gas driving all the way there. She stood regarding the sign, stalling the surrender of simply driving back home. The sun hung low in the sky, but still had an hour or two of promise. She settled back into the worn brown driver's seat of the station wagon, then started the short drive to a shoreside park near downtown instead.

She walked the Duluth boardwalk rarely, but she was familiar with the area. It would be a change of scenery from her wild Northern property; the walk was overly manicured but appealing, nonetheless. It was a wonderful temperature outside, and one had to make the most of good weather. Walking was Sarah's most dependable habit. This different route would make the wasted commute count for something. Sarah walked for a half hour on most days of the year; other nights—like this one, crisp but with the promise of summer days ahead—she might be out for an hour or more. Walking was an exercise, but also a compulsion. It kept her level, made it seem like her mind wasn't racing but instead merely spinning along with her long strides.

A light wind whistled against Sarah's bare face and blew her downy hair back. The air smelled like a crushed stem of mint. The sunlight was waning in long shadows as the sky faded to the color of late season bittersweet. The lake spread its gray vastness past the horizon. Waves crashed on the rocks below. The winding slats of the path along the ridge guided Sarah along, and her feet thumped over the wood of the boardwalk. It took her through tree-lined parks and a rose garden with arches and fountains. There were still plenty of people out and about, even as the lampposts began to come on.

As she moved down the path with hands thrust in her pockets, a man in a khaki work jacket gave Sarah a nod and a broad smile, but she didn't notice. Sarah hadn't been interested in any kind of interaction with men since sometime in her thirties, back when she was still filled with a desire to conquer the halls of academe, back when *genius* was a word used by friends and strangers alike in their descriptions of her. That was before the bad feelings, invasively persistent and intimately aware of the landscape of her mind, had arrived to infiltrate the functionality of her life. Before the paranoia had taken hold. Before she had run as far away from California as the last vestiges of the grant money could get her. Before she had withdrawn from science, changed her name, and simply dropped off the map. Now she was Sarah Turnsfield, grocery clerk from Duluth, Minnesota. Inconsequential.

She walked, long limbs driving her forward. Her light denim and green fleece made her look as unassuming as any of the Midwestern tourists who also walked the boardwalk along Lake Superior during the warmer seasons. The cries of circling herring gulls sounded high and misty in the distance. The waves rushed the boulders below, nearly in time to Sarah's strides. *As long as I am moving,* she thought, *everything is in motion. All is aligned. The planet turns. Currents flow. Ideas turn over like grains of sand and I am moving, and it is all immense and of equal value.* She gazed out over the water. It always amused her to think about how Lake Superior, one of Earth's youngest geological features, was also one of the biggest freshwater lakes in the world. Sarah looked at the lake as her sister in kind. The depths, the movement. Some days being clearer than others. The way she caught up to herself when standing still. Watching the water brush the shoreline filled her with delight.

Then, she heard the sound of bicycle tires whirring. Something was invading, shutting her joy into darkness. She spun around to locate the origin of the sound. Three high school students, maybe a hundred yards behind her, were laughing, talking, and riding slowly along.

Sarah knew that they could not logically be children of old colleagues sent to find her out. She knew that she did not hear them use her real name and call the news station to say that she had been spotted. She knew that they could not be graduate school assistants disguised in clothes a decade too young for them to catch her and bring her back to the university.

She knew; but she still could not stop herself from being overwhelmingly, viscerally convinced that any or all of these were true.

She told herself to relax, to put aside every illogical instinct and refuse to give in to the urge to run. But she could not. Like a startled rabbit, she half-bolted, half-jumped herself into a sprinting pace. She split down the boardwalk, heavy footfalls slamming the wood faster and faster as she tried to gain shelter from view.

Rounding the corner, she looked back. The bikes were rushing at her. She needed to hide, or maybe even grab a couple palm-sized rocks to defend herself, though it would do little good. She was wiry and strong, but not enough to overpower three. There was a railing between her and a drop of twenty feet to the frigid lake water, turbulent with the night wind. Though the back of her mind winced at the idea, she followed it the second it came to her—tilting her head and torso over the side of the railing, she flipped her body over the other side. Just below was a rusting metal ladder, embedded in the concrete wall. The red dust smeared her pants and sleeves as she shuffled down, banging her knee hard on the metal. *They can't find me*, she repeated in her head. *They can't find me. They can't find me.* She drew her face up against the side of the concrete. The worst moment was when she heard the bikes wheel up overhead.

"Hey!" cried a young male voice, hoarse but earnest. "Are you all right?"

Sarah clung to the ladder, unresponsive, eyes tightly closed, and face turned to the water.

"Uh . . . hey, ma'am? Are you ok?" Still nothing. They shuffled. Bikes were leaned against the railing. She heard them arguing among themselves, voices low.

"Should we call the cops? She's not moving or anything."

"I don't know. She's hanging on, though. I think she wants us to go away."

"It's not like we're gonna do anything."

"Shut up."

"Let's just leave her alone."

"We can't just—"

"Come on. This is messed up. Leave it alone." Two sped off, one lingered for a minute. Then they were gone.

Sarah hardly breathed for three minutes afterward, until she cautiously pulled herself back up, rolling up on her stomach to scoot herself forward, barely squeezing back under the railing. Her face was scraped and raw. Her thoughts searched for a mooring.

Her head swam as she righted herself and stood. Exactly what had happened, she wasn't sure. Confusion blinded her.

She did know where home was.

She did know that something like what had just happened tonight had also happened before.

She willed herself to just start walking again, steadily, forward, until she regained herself. For the first time in a long time, she wished someone else was walking along with her.

7

TRENTON FLORAL WAS BUSY ON Saturday morning. Jo worked in the back room, while Tonya and Ruth spoke with a young couple about a wedding order in the front of the store. Jo could hear the bride explicating her grand vision for the occasion, a splendor of lavender and white. The young bride burst with words and sweeping arm gestures as Tonya did what she could to insert information about pricing and delivery edgewise.

Jo, deep in her own creative flow, pressed her lips together. There is always someone about to plan the perfect wedding at a flower shop, gazing at the abundant everlasting freshness of it all. The customers never have to trouble themselves with the piles of blooms mounding in garbage bags the second they get too soft. Nothing gets a chance to die—but then, Jo thought, that's how it should be. Jo placed long stems deep into the softness of wet floral foam. She had a half hour to finish the altar arrangement for that afternoon's bridal order. So many weddings. The colors for this one, though, were especially luscious—rich jewel tones of fuchsia, violet, tangerine, cobalt, and chartreuse. Her hands wove between the thick lemon leaf and ruscus branches that formed the green frame of the arrangement, placing things just so. Her fingers spoke the language of color, stripping excess leaves with easy hands, grouping blooms together in clusters of texture, bounty spilling over the side of the piece. She nodded. It was going to be stunning.

As she arranged the flowers, her mind invented the couple who would make vows at the ceremony, and the years of marriage that would follow. She imagined herself, dressed like Ophelia in a Waterhouse painting, tossing flowers in grief, naming them for symbols. The blue delphinium, those little clusters of stars, for children. Spiky green dianthus for small, biting arguments. Asiatic lilies, their strong petals unfurled, for love-flooded forgiveness. And the lush, layered petals of peonies for the thousands and thousands of hours, devoted in fidelity, no matter the cost, to preserve the bond they swore to uphold. Everyone knew that story, because it was a good story, with a good ending. The scent in the room was heady. Sweetness ached in her nostrils: a green-spiced softness, alive and dense, like tea chilled in the ground.

The arrangement was perfectly balanced, flowers in an intuitive pattern like constellations in her own little sky of dark leaves. Jo sighed with satisfaction.

At Tonya's cue, the three women started to box up the floral pieces for the wedding delivery. Struggling to keep her bag from falling off her shoulder as she made last-minute adjustments, Ruth shouted to Jo from the front of the store. It was time to load the van. She fluffed tissue paper around a collection of packed vases that were ready to receive bouquets. Lifting each one from the cooler, Jo sighed at their tight weight and all the ribbons trailing down. She placed them just so, not one petal bruised. Tonya's high heels clicked as she carried the first box out the door. "Ready, Jo?" she asked over her shoulder.

"Be right out," Jo called back. She noticed one small hole in the composition of her altar arrangement low on the right side, a small oversight that could look like a huge one from the wrong angle. One more vibrant pink rose would fill the spot in. She bent her whole body into the cooler to reach the very back. The only roses left to use were unprocessed, long, and sitting in a bucket with flexible cardboard wrapped tightly around the heads to keep them from opening too soon. She tugged just one rose up and out from the bunch and brought it back to the counter. She reached for the knife she'd been working with and cut the stem down. The thorns were sharp as death—she needed to strip those off, too. Jo's wet hand slid the knife down the thick, woody flesh of the stem. The first four thorns dropped off, and then she slipped.

The knife sliced across the pad of her index finger, and Jo watched a thin red line appear in half a second. Cursing, she took a closer look. It wasn't too bad, but she'd need to wrap it in a waterproof bandage for the next week or so. The cut stung hard. The line of blood swelled thicker while Jo rummaged one-handedly through some drawers to see if there was a box of Band-Aids. There were none that she could find.

"We're ready to load the last one, Jo!" Tonya gave her a wave from the door. She and Ruth were taking more boxes outside on the rolling cart.

"Right behind you," yelled Jo. Her finger was dripping now, but there was no time. Holding back the fragile greens of the arrangement with one hand, she stuck the rose in. As she pulled her hand away, she saw that her blood had colored the very bottom of the rose head, but with a couple leaves pulled forward underneath, there was no way anyone would see it. Jo scrunched a paper towel around her bleeding finger, just as Tonya came back in to help her carry out the large arrangement.

"You cut yourself?" Tonya asked.

"Yeah, it's nothing," said Jo, and she laughed. The blood seeped through the paper towel. She clenched down harder.

"Don't worry—I've got bandages in the van." She and Jo lifted the piece up together.

LATER, AT THE church, Jo's face hurt from smiling at all the loveliness, the family, the bustling, the polite sympathies for her fat, bandaged finger as she pinned boutonnieres into jacket lapels. It was strange to have access to such intimate family moments, for people she hadn't even met before. Trust filled the room, thick as the afternoon sunlight radiating through the high church window. Tonya made sure everything looked perfect and set resplendent bouquets into the hands of gasping women in delicate gowns. Once everything was ready, Jo waited in the back of the atrium with Tonya and Ruth just long enough to see the bride—young and fragrant—enter the sanctuary and start down the aisle, white silk whispering along behind her. The bride's back, graceful, with one beauty mark to the left of a shoulder blade, spun the room into melody.

The wood of the long benches creaked as the congregation on both sides rose to their feet. "Shit," whispered Jo, raising a wrist to her face. Her throat stung with how beautiful it all was.

8

HOWARD KNEW HE WAS LOSING money with each desperate day that he didn't leave his bed. When he found himself in the kitchen one morning, scraping the bottom of a bowl of oatmeal, he inwardly celebrated the fact that he had started to eat again. He was starting to worry about his work. He wasn't sure what to do to get his head, much less his monstrous body, back to right. The panic still found him, but he wasn't passing out from it anymore. The practical part of Howard's mind counted the days that he had been transparent, but still hadn't died. Three.

In those three days, Howard began to grow strangely accustomed to the sight of his gruesome hands. He simply avoided the rest. He looked up to the ceiling when he finally undressed for the first time. In the shower, he kept his eyes shut tight, just focusing on the warmth of the water holding him safe. He told himself that all of this could be an elaborate sustained hallucination. He thought of the long decade of therapy that defined his childhood, and the bloody man he'd seen in the woods came ringing back. He remembered his mother, with her light, always-haphazard hair, stroking his forehead mechanically each night before bed, saying *there's no such thing, your imagination tricked you, he isn't real*. She never looked at him when she said those things. But he was convinced, just as he was now. He was a serious child, not given to fancy, at least not until that first evening playing in the yard at twilight, when he thought he saw a man without skin at the back of the lot. It was only for a moment, but the skeletal red face contorted. It had looked at him, struck him with an all-encompassing fear. But he was only a child, and his mother reassured him, sang it to him like a litany in her tired voice at his bedside. It was something he left untouched in his memory, never told anyone. He hadn't had any more trouble like that since moving out at eighteen. Once he moved out, got his own place, and set up routines he could trust, he stopped seeing things that were untrue. At least, that's what he had thought.

But now? He saw the skinless man's hands, real as ever, before him. They were his hands.

Howard confronted his skin's transparency, and the mosaic of muscle and vein visibly sliding beneath it, standing before the vanity in the bathroom. Even as he tried to avoid it, the mirror hissed to him of darkened dreams. He tried to watch his face, honestly, in the mirror, until the vision eroded. He hoped, if this was some hallucination left over from his lonely boyhood, that he could make himself see the truth. If he focused enough, if he remained calm, if he looked long enough, it would disappear.

The fear built up like sour bile. He approached the sink gingerly, keeping his eyes on the drain. When he raised his chin and looked forward, he could only do it for a moment before a long ugly sound tore from his throat. He could do nothing but think the word *no*, breathing quick, eyes back on the drain, hands gripping the sides of the sink. With his eyes closed, the walls of the bathroom fell away. There again, in the imagined distance, there was the mirage of a blood-drenched man stalking among the thick trees of his childhood home at the edge of the woods. He could hear the echoes of patient concern, this time in his father's voice, talking him down. Damn if the mind isn't inventive, Howard thought. But when he opened his eyes, he saw the same torque of red muscle stretched over his skull. There was the same cheekbone white shining through beneath his startled eyes.

This was no night terror or waking dream.

It was as real as rain, and he knew it.

He decided to tack up a spare bedsheet over the mirror.

Starting with the upper left corner, he nailed the fabric down. His clear fingernails grew redder with the pressure of his fingers holding the nail to the wall, waiting for three brisk hits with the hammer. Howard's work was done with care. He didn't want to leave any gashes in the drywall.

Howard sat at his small kitchen table, spine curled forward, weary with fear. He needed to talk to someone. It was such a rare thought for him, but these were rare circumstances. He scrolled through his contacts. They were few and far between. His friendships tended steeply toward the casual, which was just as well. There was Rob, who he knew from the part-time work he used to do at a loading dock. There was Nate, his journalist friend who wrote for the *Sun-Tribune* now. But he rarely talked to either of them, not about anything personal. His mother was completely out of the question. Howard kept scrolling back to the same name, and as much as he tried to find an alternative, there wasn't one: it was still Tiffany.

He pressed "call."

As the phone rang, Howard cursed himself for the hundredth time for yielding so easily to the idea of parting ways with Tiff. She was his last and most serious relationship, but it ended two years ago. He'd been enchanted by her wit and ease in all situations, and she by his, well, what had it been? Whatever it was, it didn't last. He remembered sitting down with her on the curb outside her house, as if they were fourteen-year-olds, each dancing delicately around the idea and laughing in relief when they both agreed that the relationship wasn't going anywhere. Tiff, with her green eyes and long body—she was too good for him. Too good for this world, really, which was probably why she still picked up when he called, including this time.

"Hey, Howard," she said, the upturned mischief of her lips audible in her voice. He closed his eyes. He couldn't respond. Her voice sounded so entirely normal. As if everything was as it should be. He could imagine her pulling her light hair over to one side like she always did.

"Howard?" she asked into the silence. "Are you there?"

"I'm here," he said. *I'm here*, he thought. *I'm here.*

"Oh good, I thought I lost you there for a second! How are you, you cad?"

He smiled, insisting he was anything but a cad. He kept the truth vague, but he told her what he could. He wasn't feeling well, he said, just needed to hear someone's voice, he wasn't himself. She listened and questioned and empathized. They had always been good at caring for one another, even when the attraction faded. And for all Tiffany's performative flair, she took these kinds of things very seriously.

"Do you want to come out for a drink or something?" she asked. "Really! We could go right now! Jules won't care, he knows I'm half feral."

Howard declined, but he asked if she wouldn't mind just staying on the call with him for a while, until he felt steadier. They talked about their disastrous past dating lives, how they were both still not talking to their parents, and how remarkably beautiful Duluth was in the spring.

"It's better from the east end, though," she said. It was a perennial debate. Howard waited until the cadence of the conversation reached its natural end, at which point he yielded that yes, she must be right about that.

"I missed talking to you," he said. "I'm so sorry to intrude on your evening like this, but I have to tell you how much I appreciate it. I feel renewed."

"I'm glad. I'm glad we're still friends."

"Me too, Tiff."

"Just don't get any ideas, OK? I'm practically engaged to this madman over here." Howard could hear Jules yelling "Hey!" in the background as

Tiff dissolved into laughter. "Take care of yourself," she said, her unique brand of kindness radiating from the other side of the connection.

"I will."

"Sure you're OK?"

"Yes. Thank you so much for this. I owe you." She scolded him a little and bade him goodbye.

Howard set his phone down and just looked at it, waiting for his feelings to fall into a shape that made sense. He felt like the faded sketch of reality had been colored back in. He was real again, and so could move forward. She had always been so wonderful to him, he thought, even in all his failings. That was years ago. How long had it been since he'd seen her in person? How long since he'd seen anyone? He couldn't remember. Probably his mother, over a year ago, briefly, at the holidays. He squeezed one hand with the other, trying to warm it.

He stormed the keyboard with search queries, looking for information about anything close to his condition. If anyone out there in the world had experienced this same thing, he told himself, there would be something online about it. He kept finding information about a group of skin conditions, a specific inherited syndrome. But that was just one of many. There were threads and social media accounts from people with all kinds of debilitating conditions—bruising at the lightest touch, cuts that couldn't heal, skin that was cystic and inflamed. He read medical articles from the academic database he subscribed to as a work expense. But nothing he could find record of came close to resembling the way his body's grotesque workings shone through his crystalline skin, clear as a rocky riverbed beneath pristine water.

He kept searching. He focused on treatments. But almost all the skin conditions he found online, even as mild as they were compared to his, involved lifelong management and medical therapy. Nothing was said of permanent treatment, of cures. He looked down at the notepad next to him where he'd started keeping pencil recordings of his temperature, fluid intake, and sleep cycles. A worthless catalog. He was far beyond his depth. Howard had a plunging sense that nothing would put this new reality back into the hole from which it had sprung. His body sweetened in response to the thought, blood rushing the surface, the scent of cinnamon invented from nowhere.

He found a roll of black electrical tape in the back of his desk drawer. He snipped off a piece with scissors and smoothed it over his webcam. Nobody would ever need to know about any of this, he thought. Something else entered his mind.

He had to get it together enough to start writing again. He needed to keep his income flowing. He straightened up where he sat, lifting his sternum, feeling his vertebrae stretch into place and his shoulder blades drop, pulling his shoulders back. He lifted his chin, loosened his jaw. He brought up his email. His crimson fingers swept across the touchpad as he started sorting through leads.

9

THE SATURDAY EVENING LINGERED WITH humidity in the humming fluorescent light of Ahlborn's. Sarah sprayed cleanser over the conveyor belt and wiped it down for the fifth time since the start of her shift. It was the light that she hated most about her workplace. That clean, industrial glow reminded her too well of places that used to mean so much to her. Sometimes on these slow nights, the sound of the looping soft rock on the store's speakers seemed to fade out. The decades replayed mercilessly in her mind.

Her most distressing memories were always of her time at the university, the late 1990s. They were years of golden promise. She was a loved commodity then, for human interest reporters and societies for the advancement of science alike. Success seemed an inevitable arrival point for her. She perpetually chased the high of academic discovery. Scientific work had a purity of patterns that, to Sarah, was like a glowing white landscape. Just her, alone with the effects, the data, her findings. Her mind craved the efficiency and thrill of this interior space, and she pursued it with a startling boldness.

The mixture of Sarah's uncanny beauty, her outspoken declarations about her field's progress, and a razor-sharp mind made the media glow when she—a researcher with doctorates in botany and evolutionary biology—became prominently swept up in early attempts to administer gene therapy in human clinical trials. Her work was groundbreaking: she translated techniques used to genetically modify plant crops into approaches for work in lab animal populations. Later, she would consult on the development of methods used to administer gene therapy to human patients.

Her early work was elegant. She found immense success. She could make freshwater fish phosphorescent. She could liquefy bulbous lab rat tumors. She saw genetic predispositions as suggestions that could be rewritten. She understood DNA and the design of viral vectors like a sculptor understands the nuance of metal, wire, and stone. She published a paper that claimed—radically—that one day, carefully engineered and administered gene therapy could make certain species of fish and amphibians practically immortal, and that humans would follow. Regeneration was nearly limitless in her eyes, and in the eyes of the public. A future where inherited disease was merely a memory seemed foreseeable. Sarah served as the face of her contemporaries in a six-page article in a 1998 issue of *Time*. It opened with her portrait, sun illuminating her blond, windswept bangs like a halo as she stood in front of Mercy Hospital in San Francisco, a team of doctors and researchers behind her. The title "Angels of Mercy" graced the top in an elegant serif font. Human trials had begun by the time the issue hit the stands.

Before that article was published, Sarah spent her evenings sitting on the back porch watching the sun go down, with the jacaranda trees and sea lavender bathing the air in violet. She would think about the patterns of the future, imagining she might see them in the swoop of a thrush. But afterward, it was all different. Angry mail began to pour in. It would inundate her mailbox at work and soon, inexplicably, her home. How they had gotten her address, she had no idea. At times, well-articulated arguments about the ethical implications of reorganizing genetic code held her attention until the fluid signatures at the bottom. Equally as often, she tried not to look at the folded, handwritten papers covered unevenly with violent messages before stuffing them in the trash. She dismissed the threats consciously; they were ridiculous. But she began to look over her shoulder when she went out. She felt shaky. The letters kept coming.

Even while eating dinner with her research colleague and boyfriend, Tom, she would look constantly to the side, too distracted to eat, wondering whether some zealot would take that evening as his opportunity to punish her for reorganizing the laws of nature. Her pristine landscape was no longer a haven because she could no longer find the sense of solitude she required to see the patterns that underlaid it. She became distracted. When she entered the lab, she imagined faceless people entering the lab in disguise, ready to sabotage their work. She remembered asking Tom if he thought people were following them, if he thought they were a threat.

"Those people have nothing to do with what we're doing," he said, taking her small hand in his hand, and nudging her untouched glass of chardonnay a few centimeters closer to her. "It will all be worth it. The history of medicine is changing in front of our eyes. Sick kids, Sarah. We're going to save the lives of children who never had a chance before. We have to focus on that. We're going to give life where there once was nothing, no chance." Her blue eyes would spark for a moment, but she could feel her trust in him shine a little less each time. It was a conversation they'd have again and again.

Tom wanted to help people. But for Sarah, people were an uncomfortable complication to the work she loved. She tried to bolster her old conviction. Even when it scared the hell out of her, she joined Tom and others from the team in damage control, publicly defending their work, with grace, to panels and editorialists. Around the same time, human trials began—a tangible result of all their research. Several hopeful adult volunteers who suffered from genetic conditions were looking for cures. It was happening across the country with other teams, too. The threshold was about to be crossed, and bodily evidence provided by lab animal tests indicated that marked success could be a near-immediate result, rocketing genetic therapies into practice worldwide.

The months that followed brought mixed results, with certain side effects starting to manifest that the researchers hadn't expected. Still, the work seemed very promising.

And then a trial patient in Pennsylvania died. A young person who, other than requiring a daily cocktail of pills, had been perfectly healthy and functioning before he'd volunteered to test the miracle treatment of gene therapy.

Two more patients in San Francisco died too. Sarah read the reports—a thirty-two-year-old female with sickle cell anemia. Urine turned black. Bruises spread like ink droplets in water. Lungs became too fragile to function. The exact pitch of that patient's monitor flatlining was one that Sarah imagined she heard for a long time afterward, even though she hadn't been there to hear it. She wasn't a doctor, of course, had never touched a patient. But the threats that she feared were now so much more than an intrusive thought here and there. The public outcry raged in her subconscious. She started envisioning an escape route, away from the science, her spoiled haven, the boyfriend she'd thought she'd wanted, the city itself. She thought that she had contributed real answers. Now people were dead, in part because of her detached confidence, her hands in the lab. Her numbers. Her ideas. The flatline sound danced its way across her brain, irreversible and electric. The San Francisco breeze turned cold.

Words like *promise*, *groundbreaking*, and *angels* disappeared from the media voice. Everyone involved in the trials was advised to keep the patient deaths as quiet as possible, so that moving forward was still an option. That was when Dr. Kristen Telfel—it was her name at that time—started to die, too; a willing death of a unique mind, a brilliant identity. That person was accessible to Sarah now only in moments of sincere self-confrontation, and only in brief flashes. At least she'd told

Tom goodbye, even though he hadn't recognized it for what it was. The last night they slept together. When he didn't find her the next day, she was already out of the state. As she bolted down the freeway in a rental car, the idea emerged fully formed. What if she could start over? Just her and the faultless interior landscape of her mind. No connections. No complications. No relationships. No threats. Her hungry mind seized on the challenge. She started working out how to accomplish it.

She orchestrated ways to stay adrift and separate from her former life. Every few years, she moved to a new city, straying farther and farther away from anything that was recognizable. It was remarkably easy to disappear for an intelligent, desperate person willing to withdraw from all social contact. She managed a scheme where she innocuously stole her own identity in order to be assigned a new Social Security number. She changed the name she went by. She paid for nearly everything in cash, and she stuck to renting places where either ineptitude or indifference caused landlords to offer a lease without a credit check. The more parts she sponged out of the person she used to be, the less she felt the constant press of warning. It was a new kind of hollow satisfaction, a clear and decisive pulling up of her life's anchor. She let it all fall away. She would always have her mind. She wondered how much of the rest of it she could remove.

The system wasn't foolproof—she had been recognized and stopped at least eight different times. In her second month on the run, her sister had found her and pleaded with her to come home, following an anonymous report that someone fitting her missing-person description had been seen buying fruit at a farmers market near Phoenix, Arizona. Tom mounted a search for her a year later that ended in a fraught confrontation at a Chicago women's shelter where Sarah had stayed for a time. She refused his help, and he left in frustration.

After repeated bitter rejections and ceaseless running, she was safe. The people she used to call family and friends let her stay missing. They didn't talk about her. They stopped setting an empty place for her at holidays, and hoped that somewhere she was still alive, and living well. As time always does, it made the situation normal, or something like it.

Now, as Sarah massaged a rag over the sticky part of the Ahlborn's conveyor belt, she hazarded short thoughts about the people that used to comprise her world. What did Tom look like now? Was her mother still living in the house on Vesper Drive? Had either of her sisters had more children? Did any of her old colleagues even remember her name? Or was she just thought of as that woman who had gone mad and disappeared? It was less like thinking and more like the shifting glimmers of feeling after a dream. None of it felt real.

She was jolted back to the present moment when the reliable, muffled sound of the night manager's voice boomed out over the Saturday night intercom. Hearing him now, she sighed and centered herself. Keith's voice warmly invited customers to consider the seasonal picnic display.

Sarah watched Keith put the receiver down from behind the service counter. He laughed out a syllable, then cleared his throat. When he saw Sarah watching him, he came around the desk and walked up to her register.

"I don't know how many people are having picnics at eleven at night," he said, punctuating with a low chuckle. "But hey—that's the copy of the hourly announcement that Frank wrote this morning, and hell if I'm going to change it now." The one customer in the store glanced over briefly with a smirk, then disappeared into an aisle. Keith pushed up the dark-framed glasses that were sliding down his nose and clasped his hands behind his back. He was a portly man, chin peppered with uneven stubble. "How are you doing tonight, Sarah?"

"I am fine." Her voice was rough, objective, at the edge of masculine. "I've had twelve customers tonight." She swept her rag over the belt once more and looked up at him.

"Good to hear." Keith nodded and started straightening a shelf of mints and chewing gum. She kept her eyes down because she knew they were disarming. Hadn't she been told that so many times? Pale. Hollow. She wondered what Keith thought of her, his smile so real, albeit hesitant. She did her job well. She was always on time. She was clean and efficient. No customer had ever once complained about her. She had all the produce codes memorized for her own entertainment. But she couldn't make small talk with him. It was too bad, really. She wondered what the fabric of his red flannel shirt felt like. Rough wool, or worn and smooth. He wasn't quite close enough to tell.

"Think I have a box of labels to work on," she said. "Were they left there in the back for me?"

"Oh," he said. "I didn't notice. Let me take a look for you." His shoulder turned back toward the service desk.

"Thanks, Keith," she said, and there—right there—he might have heard a touch of sadness in the way she said his name. But no: when she looked up, just a benign nod. Any question, any mystery about her was lost on the rough-cheeked manager. Sarah wiped her palms on the thighs of her tan khakis. She cleared her throat as quietly as she could. She saw Keith coming back with the box full of labels. Soon, she'd be up to her forearms in numbers and codes. She rolled up her sleeves.

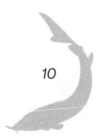

10

HOWARD JUMPED AT THE SHRILL buzz from the apartment's ringer panel. His packages had arrived. He pressed the white button by the door and talked into the speaker, heart pounding.

"Hello?"

"Hi, I got a delivery. Packages for Howard Wright. Your directions said to ring."

"Thanks, I'm in unit 13. Just leave it outside the door."

"Will do." Howard pressed the red button to buzz the man in. He heard the heavy footsteps and the bump of cardboard against his door. After a minute or two, he put on his winter gloves and shot a hand outside to slide the boxes in before slamming the door shut and replacing the brass chain lock in its slider. It was a ritual action that he also did with the bags of takeout that he had delivered for dinner most nights. The empty containers piled up in his trash.

Howard took off his gloves. He tossed them aside and started tearing into the boxes. They were filled with cosmetics. He'd ordered them after finding a link on one of the medical articles he was reading, which led to a video of a woman with severe rosacea that flamed across her nose and cheeks. She was using makeup to conceal her flare-up, moving and blending dabs of color across her face like she was her own painting. Howard was transfixed as he watched the redness slowly disappear and the woman's face transform. He picked up a pen and imitated the action of her hands alongside the video, pretending it was the fat, feathery application brush he saw on the screen. He followed the dendrites of related links to an endless thread of video tutorials from vloggers who used pigment to create what he considered to be no less than miracles. Entirely new faces emerged. He watched for hours. He even commented personal thank you messages to those who listed their products by brand, shade, and name in the video descriptions. Sometimes he got a little heart symbol on his post in return, small automated tendernesses he took with gratitude.

He'd filled his online cart with product lines made specifically to correct redness, shocked by the price tag at the end. But if it worked, and he thought it might, he could hide the horrific truth of himself. He laughed skeptically now as he took each item out of the boxes, but the only way to know was to try. He had a methodology, some tools to work with.

Makeup crowded the faded laminate of the kitchen counter as Howard set down the various tubes, applicators, jars, brushes, and pots of pigment that came out of the boxes. He screwed off one of the lids, dipping his finger into the pale liquid makeup with a green undertone. Full coverage, it said. He smoothed the wet color on to the skin of the back of his hand. It smeared, and the red showed through in streaks like those left by a drying paintbrush. But the more foundation he spread from his knuckle to wrist, the more layers he applied with different liquids and powders in the order he had seen on the videos, the closer to normal his skin appeared. Howard daubed out a whole puddle into his palm, and started spreading it over his face, starting with a large upside-down triangle pointing down from the edge of each eyelid, and grinding the color into his cheekbones, over his ears, and across his eyelids. As he felt the first layer of moisturizing concealer start to dry, he decided to hazard a look into one of the little compact mirrors that came with the makeup.

He saw his eye first, then tilted the little circle around to his jaw, nose, and lips.

It was a poor attempt, without a trace of finesse. Great globs of the foundation clumped at the ends of his eyelashes, and he'd missed several inch-wide streaks on his face. The red shone through like deep slicing cuts. The color was uneven and runny. But he saw what it could be. With practice, Howard felt hopeful that he could perfect the process, using color to smooth and pigment his face into something like what he used to look like. He took out the powder and opened it. He turned the applicator over in his hand, wondering at its lightness. He took the softer side and dabbed the smooth powder over his forehead. Looking back in the tiny mirror, he saw how the powder took off the sheen and made his skin look dry, even soft. He could maybe even go outside like this. It was sincerely remarkable how well it worked.

Every day, between hard writing sessions, he practiced along with the online tutorials. There were so many. He took notes and drew a diagram of the process to help himself remember. More boxes arrived at the door. And his writing benefitted too: His freelance queue was filling with product reviews for beauty blogs. Some companies even started sending him free samples in exchange for a feature. It made him laugh, but he found he was good at it. What the hell, he thought.

It was absurdly simple. Just cover everything up.

Each morning, waking up in his long sleeves and long pants, he'd apply the first layer of makeup to his face. That helped him stomach the glances in the small compact mirrors he needed to piece the look together. The bathroom mirror stayed covered.

The freelance work kept coming, and so did the boxes. Every day, Howard began with his makeup routine. As he went about his day, he felt safe under the heaviness of the creams and powders. He felt like he had control of the situation, until his ritual shower each night before bed. He would lock his eyes on the ceiling, washing himself by touch as fast as he could, smoothing soap over chest, down around between his legs, back up over hips and into the curve of his neck. Then he'd turn his face to the spray and feel the skin kick as the monster was freed. He couldn't stand the prick of stubble, so he'd run his razor over his chin in the water, brushing his face afterward with his palm to check for missed spots. The hot water ran in chalky beige rivulets as the makeup poured off his face and down the clear skin of his body, over the dark blood that turned beneath, over his lean shoulders, the long, elegant veins of his legs, and over the little pouch of yellow fat that cupped the curve of his belly. His body, like crystal, sang when wet.

11

ON A WEDNESDAY AFTERNOON, Jo begged a ride home from work with Ruth by way of the hardware store on Logan Avenue. Her tiny apartment needed some color. She wanted to define it, beyond the dusty smell and the scuffs of previous tenants. In the lease, it said she was allowed to paint any walls she wanted, as long as she painted it back to white before she moved. If she was honest with herself, Jo did miss the color of her old bedroom. She made a half-hearted attempt to browse through the vast wall of paint chip samples, but her heart knew that particular light blue in an instant. There was no real deliberation. After all, she'd chosen it before. Her paycheck from Trenton was decent the week before, so she was able to pick up two cans of that familiar robin's egg hue, a couple of tarps, a roller and tray. No primer. No painter's tape—she trusted her hand's steadiness. Plus, as Ruth pointed out, they were selling it for five bucks a roll. Seemed like an overcharge. Ruth dropped Jo off at her building on Second Street and waved goodbye, her hand poking up from the open sunroof of her silver hatchback.

Jo stopped at the mailboxes in the lobby, dropped the envelopes into the plastic bag from the hardware store and looped it up to her elbow to get a better grip on the paint cans as she hauled them up the apartment stairs. As she walked down the hallway, she said hello to a courier who was setting down some packages outside her neighbor's door. "This guy gets deliveries almost every day," he said. She shrugged at him and he shrugged back before being on his way. Jo glanced at the boxes, wondering what was in them. She unlocked her door.

When she got inside, Ike swirled himself around her legs, meowing, tail curled into a question mark. She put her paint supplies down and gave his chin a scratch. "Hello, sweet one," she said. She poured more food into his bowl and put fresh water in his shallow drinking dish. As she watched him submerge his snout in the food, she responded to a text message from her mother, assuring her that yes, she was doing fine. There was also a missed call from Cait, her college friend who lived in Duluth. Jo thought she'd run into Cait at the café near Trenton, but they hadn't crossed paths yet. She made a mental note to schedule that lunch date soon. She sifted through the mail. Most of it was still addressed to the previous tenant. She tossed the whole pile.

Soon the cat was sated and back to napping, and Jo used a kitchen knife to crank the lid off the first paint can. The smell was nostalgic and strong, filling the room instantly. She had to shove at the bedroom window to get it open, but it eventually came free, letting mild outside air filter in. She flicked a dead insect out of the screen. One of the mismatched kitchen chairs would do in lieu of a ladder, she thought. The roller handle extended long enough for her to reach the ceiling. She went to the kitchen and grabbed a plastic cup. She dropped two ice cubes in, followed by the soothing dark swirl of a generous whiskey pour. Returning to shut the bedroom door, she set to her evening's work.

It wasn't that she couldn't be in the company of her family right now if she had wanted to be. She would have been welcome at her parents' house for as long as she needed. She could have stayed another year at the marketing firm, continued to go to the same restaurants with the same friends. In doing so, she could have dared Joshua to be the one to leave town instead. But even after she walked out of their home for the last time, she could still feel it holding her. She felt everything from her whole life in Colesburg grasping like a tangle of rushes around an ankle in swift water. She had kicked up, north, just trying to breathe. She did miss her family; she knew they didn't understand her choice to move so far or so quickly, at least not without a solid plan. This was an aberration in the visage of calm reason that had always defined her life.

But it was because of things like just the day before, when she received her first text message from Joshua since filling out the initial divorce paperwork—"I'm sorry, Jo. I didn't mean anything by it." She reread it three times. She felt his words bind her limbs, paralytic. There was the dragging dread, as fresh as ever.

Those nine words carried the same kind of detached appeasement that had solidified their seven years together. You didn't mean anything by what, Joshua?—she thought, eyes narrowing as she filled the tray with paint—by knowing me? By marrying me? By sharing a mortgage with me? Or by leaving me? She cussed as she felt her eyes and nose fill up at the thought. She waited for a moment, for the breeze from the open window to call her back. She could hear Ike patiently scratching at the closed bedroom door from the other side.

It's all right, she told herself. You didn't know. You loved him, and it's that simple. She kept painting. Over and up, smooth, and down. Sidestep. Again.

She painted and painted. The mechanical motion made space in her feelings for an intrusive upwelling of the things she had loved.

Joshua's vanilla skin. The way he bent in concentration over the stovetop, ever precise with chicken breasts and marinades. His sharpness. Even the apologizing, waking her up with beer on his breath, sorry that he had left her alone. The frantic thrusting that would follow only once in a great while, rough and lasting. Jo blinked for each memory, just as it came into full view, as if advancing a set of slides. She tried, hard, to recall why she had loved each of those little things so much in isolation, when the sum of her marriage to Joshua had been so profoundly lonely.

It was a mudslide of a union that she'd walked into, trusting and aglow, as if toward a holy light.

I can't fix it anymore, she thought. She knew she couldn't. But she could get her fucking walls the right color. Between deep drags from the plastic cup, ice melted now, she finished the long wall, and the room was already changed. While she was looking at it, wondering if she'd made a mistake, a sour pain spread across Jo's abdomen like a string of streetlights switching on at dusk.

Her heart surged. She edged the cat away as she slipped out the door, walked quickly to the bathroom, yanked her jeans down, and grabbed a wad of toilet paper to crush up between her legs. Fearful hope ran through her. Please, she thought. This time, it has to be. When she pulled the tissue up, it was unmistakable—a rich, red stripe of blood covered the center. Thank you, she thought. God, thank you. Thank you. Thank you. There, clutching a bloody crumple of paper, crouched on the toilet, and letting the sobs start to shudder her ribcage, Jo offered up the most earnest prayer of her life. The blood was three weeks late. But it had come. There would be no son with the same thin lips. There would be no daughter with his lithe frame. And with that realization, Jo knelt and pressed her forehead to the bathroom tile. More sobs came. Everything seemed hollow and crushingly simple. She thought about the night she asked him if he wanted a child, and the day when he blurted out—over lunch—that he didn't love her. Nothing more than a deal gone wrong. We Regret to Inform You.

Jo got up, burning in rage and relief, and collected herself. She cranked the knob on the old garage sale radio she had plugged into the wall. Sound consumed the apartment. She went to the kitchen to splash more whiskey into the plastic cup and took it back to the bedroom with her. She rested it on the hobbled end table, a small puddle forming instantly on the wood beneath it. She was determined to finish the paint job. She moved the roller across the drywall with tensely coiled strokes.

Insistent electric guitars and a raspy voice crackled through the radio speakers. She knew the song, but felt it for the first time, blood pounding and dark clouds, black lashes squinted tight, lips and teeth pressing hot breath to the metal surface of the microphone, screaming and snarling with wanting to be held. Jo kept painting, blue lines left by her roller meeting together, sweeping across the walls. She imagined the drummer's arms and long hair flying as he drove the beat forward, barely in control. She felt the expansive sunset sound that reverberated through the final verse.

Closing her eyes, tapping out the last drops of liquor stuck along the ridge at the bottom of the cup, she took in the smell of the paint with a long inhale.

Barely audible in the swell of the radio, Jo's cell phone began to ring. A brief look at the screen and she saw the word "Dad" blink at her twice. She put the phone down. They knew she was safe. They knew what city she was in. There was nothing else to say.

12

SARAH'S CABIN STOOD, CLOSELY SURROUNDED by aspen trees, a half hour north of Duluth by car. It was on an unmarked gravel road, and it was difficult to find. The house was sparsely furnished, unadorned, efficient. The space might have belonged to anyone. Sarah kept it that way by design. She cleaned behind every movement, a wet cloth over the counter almost before oil spattered from the stove. In case she ever needed to leave quickly, she could load the station wagon until it was full, and the cabin would look like nothing more than an abandoned vacation home fallen into disrepair. She had planned it out twenty-eight different times. Other than the essentials of life—a coffee maker, plates and cups, her pillow—most of her things were kept in boxes, ready to go. In the corner of the bedroom, she allowed herself four volumes of natural history reference that she kept stacked atop each other in a neat pile.

The books were simply made—plain buckram covers with foil-lettered titles in capital letters. She'd had them since college, and even as heavy as they were to carry, as relatively useless as they were when one's belongings had to fit in only so many boxes, she had managed to hold on to them all this time. For some years, they'd lain dormant along with other miscellanea in a cheap storage locker—that was when she was more transient, before she'd gotten settled here in Minnesota and was able to go back to fetch them. They'd sustained some minimal damage:

a musty smell, wrinkled waterlines on the edges of some pages. But all the text was still there. Through these books, Sarah had her own precious and tangible black-and-white record of North American flora and fauna, even of the history of the earth's constant remaking itself with rock, water, glacier, and heat. Sarah's fingers would linger on the illustrated figures as she worked through each page to memorize Latin names: genus, species. Two names for every living thing. Three when including the common name. Sometimes more. She liked knowing each name of what something was called.

She lifted the red book, the largest, off the top of the pile. The worn spine yielded easily as she cracked the book open, first moving larger sets of pages and then the individual ones, tissue-thin as they were, to find the 600-page mark. She gently extracted three sheets of parchment paper from the back of the book, each one folded in half, where she had left some early flowers to dry a few weeks ago. *Anemone nemorosa. Galanthus nivalis. Sanguinaria canadensis.* She peeled the parchment back just enough to check on each one. They were perfectly preserved, colors dulled, but shapes as defined and recognizable as ever. She smiled, and set them aside, turning to the page that held the description for each one. The petal shapes and the way leaves hung on their stems matched up to the references like blueprints.

Perhaps, she thought, one day she could hang them in the windows, in frames between two pieces of glass to catch the sun, a cross section of northern botanical life. They came from something rooted. They were a testament to another year in the woods, peaceful and without incident. For now, she placed them back in the book, but sighed. Despite her intentions, she was feeling more bound to this soil with every season.

13

LATE ON A WEEKEND MORNING, Howard felt his cosmetics techniques were finally reaching significant proficiency after all his diligent practice. He checked his handiwork, tilting the tiny circle of the compact mirror, inspecting his face inch by inch. His eyelids were growing accustomed to the reassuring heaviness of liquid and powder. The side of his mouth turned up in a reluctant smirk. The shapes of his face had a new, immediate geometry. The strong, slightly bent nose. The straight jawline. The soft, deep space beneath his eyes. He still looked maybe a shade too pale, perhaps a bit ill or undernourished, but he looked like an ordinary man from the neck up. At least from afar, he had confidence that he wouldn't be immediately noticed. The makeup stained his fingertips, standing out like paint spatter on the red canvas of his narrow hands. The meticulous application process was starting to become second nature, part of the inevitable rhythm of his life.

He allowed himself the hope that he might one day soon be able to go outside, briefly, with his face concealed like this. He could easily cover up the rest with clothing. He was sure, examining his reflection yet again, that he looked—certainly not handsome, but—at the very least not alarming. Staying under the cover of darkness would probably be best. He was so thankful that he could get everything he needed delivered. Last night, he'd risked a midnight trip to haul his garbage to the dumpster next to the building. He went quickly. Seeing and hearing no one in the hall, he shakily gathered the eleven days' worth of mail that had accumulated in his mailbox and rushed back to his apartment like his life depended on it.

He knew that some people remained shut up in their houses for great swaths of their living years. Neighbors may suspect something odd about the person living inside the unkempt house on the corner, but nobody sees inside until after a death or a foreclosure, when a landlord or family member finally bears witness to the piles of hoarded newspapers or the dirty wallpaper peeling from the corners. But for years before that, the shades can be drawn. Nobody sees, he thought. Not really. How long could he hide if he wanted to? Maybe it was far longer than he supposed.

His thoughts turned to an old movie he'd seen as a kid. He saw the 1980 film *Elephant Man* while sitting before the gray glow of the family television one night when his parents were out. The previous movie on the channel was over, and the intro credits for the next started to roll. He had nowhere to go, stretching out those long, summertime colt legs of youth on the brown carpet, trying not to feel alone. It was a hot summer night. He remembered how the air smelled, how the ceiling fan shook above him as it whirred on the highest setting. He'd never seen a movie in black and white before. Right away, he knew he didn't like it, but he couldn't stop himself from watching. His stomach soured seeing Anthony Hopkins' eyes glisten with tears, seeing the man with the swollen face contorted beyond all comprehension. It was the bag that the Elephant Man wore over his head that scared Howard the most. He imagined the scratchy, suffocating smell of the fabric, the cyclopic black hole his only portal to the world, listening to other people arguing over his future, his humanity, what he deserved or understood. Certain things about the film stayed with him. Folds of flesh on a giant head. The choking sounds of the man's sobs. It was overwhelming. Now, Howard's own life tended closer to that canvas bag than he could have imagined. But he could never allow anyone to spectate his suffering. No. If it came to that, he would find a way to end things. Then they would have his body, he supposed, but not himself. What a thing to wait for, he thought.

He couldn't let himself cry and let an hour of delicate work on his face bleed away. He tensed his throat, willed it back and down.

He heard the door open to the apartment across the hall. Before he knew what he was doing, he got up and brought his eye to the door, peering out the small peephole to see what was going on. Any distraction was welcome. He wondered what a normal person was doing while he was here living this impossibly strange nightmare.

He saw a woman heading out of unit 15. He thought she must be a new tenant—he hadn't seen her before but had been vaguely aware of someone moving in not too long ago. She looked to be about his age, maybe a year or two younger. She walked past with a light step. She had short black hair, a hugely oversized tote bag, and a cheerful cherry-red sweater that matched her lipstick. She reached in the bag and pulled out her headphones, nestled them in her ears and smiled to herself. She was so fresh and bright that Howard's heart plummeted. A month ago, he might have been brave enough to hazard a smile at her if he ran into her in the hallway. She walked out of view, and his hair fell down across his forehead.

He needed to work.

He pounded the side of his fist once against the door and walked to his desk. He needed structure. Something to move the mind and fingers, drive purpose into the day. He straightened a pile of notes on product reviews and shifted them to the side of the desk. But nothing came to him. Opening the desk drawer, he reached down to grasp for the smooth gray stone he always kept there. He'd collected it, maybe a year ago now, from the beach near the apartment. It was remarkable how round it was. It helped him think, turning the smooth surface of the stone over in one hand while the other hand sat still. He watched the cursor blink.

14

JO WALKED NORTH, ABSENTMINDEDLY OBSERVING passersby, letting her mind sweep over other things—the cool, damp morning air, the sound of cars rolling past, and her afternoon ahead at the floral shop. She thought about the immensity of Lake Superior, always there just over the hill, and wondered about the creatures that circled and perched in its underwater topography. She thought about the seething, fragile anger that scurried inside her chest. She thought about her family. She wondered if she had gotten herself lost on purpose, carefully, safely, and not quite all the way. Almost no one here knew who she was—that was the important thing. She was still herself, but without the associations. Here, Joshua had never existed. This place, the utter northernness of it, the great bridged highways, the tall pines and the dark red rock, had already started expanding inside the hollows that were left from her years of pretended indifference. She knew that everyone back home must think her great escape was evasive and childish. But she couldn't care about that. She was going to lunch.

As Jo pushed open the door of the café, a large, solid-silver bell clanked against the glass. She'd been in to order food a couple times before, but she hadn't happened to see her friend Cait yet. That was set to change today, and Jo couldn't wait. She took in the busy walls, graced with a mixture of old bicycle wheels and vintage pinup posters.

People jumbled in a loose line in front of a fifties-style diner counter. A familiar willowy redhead with a bandana tied up in her hair spotted Jo from behind the register. "Hey!" Jo broke into a smile and gave a wave. Cait looked exactly the same as she had back in college, with just a little more roundness about the hips. She wore it well. Jo checked her watch—two minutes to eleven—and saw Cait disappear back into the kitchen. Craning her neck to see the chalkboard with the soups and sandwiches of the day, Jo couldn't help but wonder how she must look through Cait's eyes. She re-tucked her T-shirt into her pants and adjusted her cherry-red cardigan to lay more squarely on her shoulders. The soothing voice of a public radio station DJ pumped out from the restaurant's sound system.

The bustling line of customers moved forward efficiently. Jo placed her order for a roast beef sandwich on wheat with swiss, cucumber, and sprouts. She took her metal table number just in time to see Cait stride out from behind the counter. Cait wrapped her arms around Jo in a stronghold of an embrace. Customers dodged past them to get to their tables, but Jo melted into the hug for as long as Cait would hold her. She laughed. Cait took a step back, then, and gave her a long look.

"My sweet Josephine!" The wattage of Cait's smile nearly knocked Jo over. It was like they were twenty-one again, seeing each other back in the dorms after Jo's long summer in Iowa. Seeing Cait felt like home. It was strange, like time hadn't passed, and life just rearranged the same props on a different set. Wisps of Cait's red hair escaped her bandana and caught the light.

"Hello, Caitlyn Leigh," said Jo. "You look incredible. This place is incredible. God, how are you? Should we get our table?"

"Yes, I reserved the corner booth just for this blessed reunion." Cait led Jo over to the big corner booth and the two women bubbled over with words. Cait was a busy woman. She took over running Rosemary Café by family necessity, after her aunt's stroke had left her disabled. After a year of learning, Cait now fit the role like a latch clicking into place. She loved the work. She was paying off her loans. She was happy. She was single but dating actively. Nothing serious, though. She had missed Jo.

A waitress brought their sandwiches out, setting the green ceramic plates down lightly, and placing two lemonades neatly beside them. Jo volunteered to fetch them some napkins and silverware. Somehow the divorce hadn't come up yet. Small miracle, thought Jo. But then, as she sat back down, of course it did.

"I hope I'm not overstepping by asking this, but are you seeing anyone new yet?"

"No, no." Jo's face burned red. "I mean, I'd like to, maybe. I'm still adjusting to things. And our final hearing isn't until September. Technically, legally, Iowa says we're still married until then."

"Shit—I didn't realize."

"Yeah. Mandatory ninety-day waiting period before the courts will legally sever the marriage. And the court date doesn't always match up with that exactly. I guess they want to give you time to know you're sure. But forget all that." Her lips made a strained line. "It'll be fine. I am liking the city, being on my own. It's good for me, I think." Jo went silent then, focusing hard on refolding her napkin. Cait's face wrinkled up in concern. She reached a hand across the table.

"Listen," said Cait, "If you really want to have a good summer, you need to head up the shore every chance you get when the weather's good. It's stunning. The lake, the hiking—it's very healing. There is nothing like it anywhere on earth. I could take you up sometime if you like. Or there's this outfitter on Barstead Street, pretty near your apartment, actually— they are fantastic. Used to tourists and newbies. They would love to tell you everything about the area, the accessible places to check out. And the secret ones." She took a sip of her lemonade. "But I should warn you that you might walk out of the store with a kayak. That tends to happen. They are not only competent there, but also persuasive."

Jo looked at her friend, wondering at the way that gold light seemed to emanate from her cheeks, how utterly vibrant she was in her black T-shirt and denim. Jo felt tension release from her neck. Cait made things sound easy. "I'll get up there soon. For you. I'll send you a picture of my feet in the lake." She didn't mention that she didn't yet have a vehicle. She made a mental note to send another email about the green truck for sale in the apartment parking lot. There were so many things she still needed to work out.

"I would love that," said Cait. She took a huge bite of her sandwich and sighed contentedly. She eyed the still-slammed café counter and pointed her thumb over her shoulder at the crowd. "I gotta finish this and get back to work. My staff could use a hand." Jo nodded. Cait wolfed down the rest of her sandwich.

"You are a marvel of the universe," Jo said, tilting her head. "We should go out some night and you can point out all the guys I guess I should be talking to."

Cait nodded, mouth packed full. She raised her index finger at Jo, dabbed at her lips with her napkin and swallowed. "Fair warning, I do not drink like we used to."

"Wish I could say the same," said Jo. Cait raised her eyebrows at that. Jo shrugged.

"You devil, you." They walked together back up to the front of the café. Cait slipped a black apron over her head and knotted it across her waist. "Come back anytime, Jo. All the time. I'm always here. Or you could call."

"I'll try not to abuse the privilege." Jo gave Cait a salute and went off to work. It was like she'd been plugged in. Seeing Cait rewired her—all the possibility she'd felt in her college days filtered through her uncertainty. Maybe it really was possible to begin again. She felt as bright as a red marker on crisp white paper. If she walked quickly, she'd be to work right on time.

15

HOWARD BUZZED IN THE DELIVERY man, whose voice he was beginning to recognize. He was the one who would cut off Howard's "You can leave it at the door" with an "I know." As he heard the thump of boxes, Howard reached out to retrieve them as usual. He knew from the online tracking notifications that the boxes held new makeup samples and some cleaning supplies he'd been waiting for. He set them on the table. But one of the boxes looked repacked, not polished and branded like the others. It was small, and Howard turned it over, looking for an address in the muddle of old, partially removed labels. The handwriting on the return address was familiar. Sure enough—Evelyn Wright. From Wisconsin. His mother. Howard felt cold.

He hadn't spoken to his mother in over a month. He had planned to contend with his overdue phone call as he usually did, the next time a check arrived from her in the mail. Sending a package was out of the ordinary for her. He thought about throwing it away unopened. He pictured his mother, in her ever-present woolen socks, shuffling across the creaking wood of the living room floor in the house he grew up in. He thought about her disheveled hair and her high voice, forever asking anyone she could if they were comfortable enough, if they needed something to drink. He remembered her as he most often saw her, making a full spread of food for just herself and her son, as if a whole family was dropping by, and carefully packing up each leftover portion that somehow disappeared in the night. Howard always assumed that she ate all the rest while he slept, but he could never understand how, with her body like a rail. His mother's power was one of disappearing, dissenting, and dismissing. Overproviding and still coming up short. And yet, she always wanted to hear his voice these days.

What would she think of him now, like this? The box burned in his hands. He used his multi-tool to slice a clean line through the packing tape that sealed the opening. A letter stared up at him. She'd used the whole page but all she had written was "Thinking of you." Beneath it, something waited, wrapped in crinkled white tissue paper and tied up with twine. He cut the twine and lifted out something soft and flexible. It was a pair of dish towels, each with a knitted buttonhole handle to attach to a refrigerator door or stove handle. The towels were old—he remembered them from childhood. Embroidered on the white cotton were colorful images of boats and ships: steamers, tugboats, sailboats, frigates. He touched the familiar raised outlines. For a moment he could almost see his mother's kitchen rise up around him. The buckling vinyl floor, the goldenrod appliances. It was something, he allowed, but two tea towels couldn't change so many bad years.

He remembered how he learned to lie to his mother, how much it distressed him as a boy to have to placate her when she was upset about the monsters he insisted he saw. He became the one comforting her, lighting a candle, telling her that everything was fine, that he was making progress, that he didn't watch the edge of the woods anymore. He didn't admit to taking both flashlights in the house to keep beneath his bed. One as a backup. One to point up toward the ceiling, the beam protecting him all night after he heard her bedroom door close. He pretended not to know anything about where all the batteries went and why, no matter how many she bought. He always thought it strange how she seemed to just accept that things had gone missing. It was like the extra food. Where did things go? The slow dissolution of their household items was commonplace, even expected. You couldn't count on something being there when you woke up the next morning. And when his father died, it was just one more thing gone missing and never discussed.

And yet, he was holding the dish towels she'd purchased from a vendor at the county fair back when he was a kid. After all she had lost, she was still willing to part with one more thing. He felt a wave of regret. He should tell his mother what was happening to him. Didn't he owe her the truth about what was happening to the body that once, so many years ago, had lived inside of hers?

No, he thought. No. She would despair, thinking his demons had returned. Or she would have to see the truth with her own eyes. Both options were unacceptable.

Maybe he would heal.

He needed more time. He put the dish towels back in the box. But the boats stayed with him. He felt like writing something.

HOURS DEEP INTO shipwreck history, Howard's ideas were steeping and coming into themselves. Unlike the formulaic approach he used to hasten his product reviews along to submission, Howard was taking his time researching and writing this piece. The article would be about one of his favorite topics, maritime vessels. He focused on Lake Superior shipwreck locations, thinking it would be a good pitch for some tourism outlets. And, more than anything, he wanted to lose himself in something he loved, and had always loved. Something far away from his own life. But also close, in a way.

He now had his mother's dish towels back out of the box. He spread them out on the desk, their little boats sailing across the surface. He'd also set up the three ships in bottles that he usually displayed around the house. There was the one from the bedroom, but also two more that he kept on the hutch in the entryway. He'd always meant to add more to the collection. They were such fascinating objects. His laptop glowed in the center of his miniature armada. Ships in bottles, ships on pages, ships in the inland sea—such exquisite machines. He could hear the tall waves crashing as he worked.

Dozens of resource tabs cluttered the laptop screen. He clicked through, scrolled down, and his breath caught on a black-and-white photograph from 1913. The image was blurred. It was of a huge steamer pitching hard to the left in a gale, its pilothouse wiped clean off in the squall, smudges of white waves raining down on the deck. The text on the front of the photograph was handwritten, presumably by a rescued crew member who had a 35 mm camera at the ready as the ship he boarded began to pull away from the sinking wreck.

WALDO

MANITOU ISLAND LAKE SUPERIOR

STORM OF NOV. 8–11 1913

The way nature rendered man-made crafts wretched and worthless was a historical legacy of Lake Superior. While the fate of the *Edmund Fitzgerald* was famed, hundreds of other vessels had bones lying on the still bottom of the lake, preserved in uncanny condition because of the cold, deep fresh water. Howard read account after account, pulled from the late 1800s through the 1970s. Ships were hurled into cliffsides in hundred-foot spray, some tossed toward the shore with such force that the bows impaled the trunks of waiting pines. Great rudders were broken off. Wood splintered. Steel bent and broke. Boats with failed engines drifted silently in the snow-filled darkness until the deafening crash of immovable rock shattered the spell. So many ships were lost with all hands. Over a dozen were still listed as ghost ships—their sailors interred below without any shred of their vessel yet found to remain.

Howard tried to think of what it might have been like, sailing the formidable great lake before modern navigational equipment, relying solely on a compass and boxed ship's clock. The trust in one's captain must have been absolute, to believe that one man could master the lake and see his crew safely home through any circumstance. How unexpected must it have been, to succumb to the god of cold, to be concussed, sucked below, and laid to rest slowly in a downward drift, the late rescue crews above finding nothing but lurching lifeboats with nobody in them.

And today, Howard thought, the remains of those proud ships are something for scuba-diving tourists to explore, and for the rest to read about on a sign, to point out twenty miles offshore in an approximate direction.

He started setting up his article headings, dividing maritime museums, dive sites, and overlooks by county. He admitted to himself that he saw it all as romantic, as noble—a history. But when he thought about the lists of the names of the dead, he touched the embroidered boats on the cotton of his mother's dish towels near the edge of his desk. To the ghosts of the lost hands in the lake, he offered up a whispered regret.

16

THE AFTERNOON SUN TURNED THE sidewalk glittering white as Jo came up over the hill toward Trenton. She'd been sleeping better, and seeing the brief slivers of the lake between blocks on her way to work filled her with something that flirted with contentment. She walked inside the shop and found no customers for the moment, but familiar faces working in the comfortable lull. Ruth and another designer who usually worked the early shift were meditatively wiping vases down and restocking new colors of ribbon.

"Hello!" cooed Ruth, setting her drying cloth to the side of a thick glass vase. A citrusy, sudsy smell hung in the air. She plucked a browning leaf from a hanging philodendron, snapping the stem with her fingernail.

Jo set her purse down on the counter. "Where's Tonya?"

"Oh, she's out back, opening up the greenhouse for the summer."

"Greenhouse?" Jo looked around for a door she had somehow missed in her first weeks of employment.

Ruth laughed. "It's only open during the warm months. Come around back and I'll show you." She bustled out the front door, and Jo followed. Through the alleyway between Trenton and the next building was a gravel path that led to a gray industrial door, which Ruth wrenched open with all the wiry strength of her wrists. Jo followed the older woman through a short hall that opened into the little greenhouse. Natural light filtered through the slanted glass panels of the ceiling in thick beams clouded with mossy fog. A fresh-looking shipment of large tropical plants sprawled their bold leaves against the back wall. The space echoed. She could smell the wet scent of new potting soil. Tonya was there in the center of the wide floor, wearing a green runner's top, her arms glistening with sweat as she hoisted crates and heavy bags into order.

"Welcome to paradise," called Tonya, and Jo grinned in response. Tonya breathed out a sigh, her face a picture of wholeness and peace.

"What can I do?" Jo couldn't suck in the humid, fragrant air fast enough. It was wonderfully warm. Tonya set down another crate, this one filled with watering cans and small bottles of liquid fertilizer. Her braids swayed along her back as she straightened back up.

"You're going to help me set up tonight. More plants are on the way. A lot more. We're going to be targeting indoor gardening this year. We'll have houseplants, terrariums, plants for window boxes, and especially things people can harvest—herbs, fruits, and vegetables that people can grow outside or indoors. Those were big sellers last year. We'll have some garden plants, too—potted rose bushes and lilies, things like that."

Jo moved to help Tonya with a heavy bag of soil. "Is the new delivery coming today?"

"Still a few weeks out," said Tonya. "We need to work with our plant consultant before I finalize our order. Since my expertise lies more on the design end, we hire an expert who recommends the best of what the wholesalers have to offer. She gives us tips on how hardy the plants are, which ones will have the most color or fragrance—she just knows every variety. She can tell exactly how they'll work out, even when they're brand new. And that means that I know what to sell."

Ruth shot Jo a knowing look. "She's quite the strange personality," she said, under her breath. Jo smirked. "Well, she is," emphasized Ruth as she glanced to the ceiling as if to seek out the author of her own impolite remark.

"Sorry, Ruth," countered Tonya, "you'll have to set your feelings about Sarah aside, since she'll be here in about a half hour to go through the Carthouse and Vedila-Moeller catalogues with me. Jo will help you and the others clean up and close after she finishes the rest of these shelving units."

"Oh," said Ruth, winking at Jo, "I'm sure she's a lovely person. Just a little different. I'll see you gals back in the shop later." Ruth closed the greenhouse door with a clunk. Tonya rolled her eyes.

"Is the consultant meeting you here in the greenhouse?" asked Jo.

"That's right," said Tonya, handing Jo a yellow, water-damaged assembly instruction booklet. "But you can be back here working—don't worry about us. Until she gets here, let's see how far we can get on these shelves."

The minutes passed by quickly. Tonya pulled out seven immense canvas bags full of heavy, interlocking metal shelving components. By the look of them, Jo figured the greenhouse had probably housed them for the past fifty years. She followed Tonya's example and shed her sweater. Her thin shirt underneath was already starting to cling. It was at least eighty degrees in the sun-warmed greenhouse by now, and the air was thick. Moisture beaded on Jo's forehead as she clicked the metal shelves into place. The physical labor felt satisfying. Jo enjoyed the resistance in her arms, capable and sure.

Soon enough, Jo heard Tonya's rich voice welcome the visitor in, and tried to look disinterested as she continued her shelving project. Tonya led the consultant to a small table set up with two stools and two glasses of ice water. She gestured toward Jo for a quick introduction.

"Sarah, this is Jo. She just started in May. Jo, this is Sarah."

The consultant nodded, her blue eyes cold, her mouth slack, and her gray-blond hair heavily draped on either side of her face. She wore long blue jeans and a shapeless beige blouse.

Strawberries, thought Jo.

She remembered this woman; she was the cashier from Ahlborn's who had sold her groceries the week before. So, she was more than just a strange night-shift grocery clerk. She was some kind of plant expert.

Jo thought, newly humored, about Ruth's dislike for this consultant. It made sense. If Ruth was a polka-dotted, gift-wrapped package of a person, Sarah was a plain paper bag: unassuming and undecipherable. Jo kept working, but she watched Tonya and Sarah from the back of the greenhouse with interest. At first, Sarah's expression remained at default blankness, her voice hardly deviating from a single flat tone. But she did talk. Furiously paging through the wholesalers' advertisements, she made more remarks about each plant variety than Tonya could ever hope to comprehensively record, even with her hand flying across the notepad, laying down blue ink line by line.

Behind her even brow, Sarah seemed ravenous for the work. It was as if a vast web of navigable data had sprung up in front of her eyes and she was flying through metaphysical space, navigating nodes of light, narrating the path aloud: "Esther's Glory . . . scent has been fairly bred out of these bushes, but they are compact and much more shade tolerant that they used to be. Five and Dime double tulips—these are good for window boxes. They are a designer plant, extremely long-lasting blossoms. Here. Bromeliads have never been so tiny, and these will live many years even with simple care. Hanfold Farms—good place. Their lemon trees can grow indoors easier than these other suppliers' trees." Sarah marked herbs, roses, succulents, tomatoes, pansies, and lavender. She made decisive, swift pen marks on the catalogue pages. For almost every plant she mentioned, she knew about the farm that supplied it and the lineage of the variety, down to the year of the wild plant's original domestication. As she studied and elaborated, a warmth entered her expression. Here, in the world of objective knowledge, of fronds and veins, she seemed to come alive. Jo found herself gaping in admiration at this woman's knowledge and the speed at which she distilled it.

Reminding herself to stop staring and focus on her own task, Jo became absorbed in her work in the back corner of the greenhouse. Sarah's string of words blurred out into soft, monotonous syllables of sound that floated above Jo's thoughts. The dynamic between this woman and Tonya seemed unusual. Jo could read a certain bend to Tonya's spine, a sense of tenderness toward the other woman, who was in turn so clearly lacking in social niceties. Jo didn't understand it, but it pacified her as she clicked, pounded, and slid each rusty row of tall shelving together. She barely thought about anything over the next hour. Rather, she let the sound of Sarah's voice hum below the metallic sounds of setting things into place on the shelves. Aluminum tubs, watering cans, terra-cotta pots, planters, spades. When she stepped back to inspect the rows of finished and furnished shelves, she felt dazed and satisfied.

She did not notice, until it had already happened, that Sarah and Tonya were no longer in the greenhouse. She checked her watch. Somehow, it was already close to closing time. Jo knew it couldn't have been long since they'd stepped out, so she hurried back toward the door to try to catch them for a quick goodbye. She didn't want to seem rude. She wiped her sweaty hands on her jeans and jogged toward the exit, where she saw one of Tonya's lime-green sticky notes left on the door. "Jo—" it read, "Please bring cart w/ new shovels in from back parking lot to storage room. We'll be in the shop closing up!"

Jo plucked the note off the door and walked out back to the narrow customer parking lot where the vendors dropped off shipments. The lot badly needed repaving—it was pitted and riddled with grass sprouting up from cracks in the asphalt. A large metal rolling cart loaded with zip-tied bundles of garden shovels and other tools sat near the main shop entrance. With so many breakable things in the display room, Jo could see why Tonya wanted the cart to be wheeled around outside to the storage room rather than taken through the shop—the heavy steel-blade shovels jutted out at haphazard angles over the edge, and one of the cart's wheels looked loose. Jo grasped the rounded plastic push handle and heaved the cart forward through the parking lot. It was cumbersome on the asphalt, resistant, and a little wobbly, but she could manage it. She was all the way through to the last parking space, almost to the ramp up to the greenhouse door, when a back wheel snagged on a rut beneath a patch of loose gravel.

The cart jammed, tilting the heavy load sharply. Before Jo could react, the largest cluster of shovels shot off the top of the pile and slammed heavily into the driver's side door of a brown Oldsmobile station wagon that was parked in the last space in the lot. The cart toppled to the side and crashed to the pavement, along with splayed-out bundles of garden rakes and hoes that careened their sharp metal parts into the side of the car before landing in a pile.

"Oh!" Jo's hand shot to her mouth. She scrambled to right the cart and hoist the bundles of tools back on top of it. She stood in front of the station wagon, willing the car to be unscathed, trying to whisper "it might be nothing" into being. But there was a dent that she could sink her whole hand into, and, to her dread, several long, angry scratches in the finish.

Helpless, she looked toward the door of the shop. She saw Tonya and Sarah heading toward her. With hot shame rising to her cheeks, she realized that the station wagon was Sarah's vehicle. Jo rushed to her with profuse, frantic apology, her right arm gesturing helplessly back at the cart. "Oh, Jo!" said Tonya, clearly upset. "Here, let's go on back in the shop. I'm sure we can all work something out. Trenton has insurance for things like this." Sarah just stood there.

Tears rose to Jo's eyes. "No, no." She touched Tonya's shoulder, then drew her hand back, embarrassed at having touched her. "I can't let you do that. This was me. You shouldn't have to take on extra work to file a claim because I was clumsy. I take total responsibility for this."

Tonya shook her head at Jo and went back into the shop without a word. Jo followed her.

Sarah stared at the car with what seemed like mild interest for a moment before joining the other women inside.

17

INSIDE THE SHOP, SARAH WATCHED as Tonya handed Jo a note-pad and gave her a quick questioning look. Tonya's lips creased as she pursed them. "Jo, I'll take a look at our liability insurance policy in case you change your mind. Really, something like this may be covered." Tonya returned to her desk, breathed in, and started typing briskly. Redness erupted across Jo's face. Sarah looked silently back and forth from Jo to her dented vehicle in the back of the lot, framed through the shop's side window. She heard Tonya clearing her throat.

"I don't know what to say, Sarah," said Jo, stumbling over the sentence, "This is my fault, not the shop's, and I should make it right. I don't have my insurance information with me. I don't even have a car right now. I mean, I'm trying to buy one, but . . . does car insurance even cover something like this?" The words coming out of Jo's mouth seemed to Sarah like they were coming out in the wrong order. She didn't look at Jo; the closest she could manage was somewhere just over her left shoulder.

"Not necessary," Sarah said. "That car is old and paid for. I'm not concerned about it. A dent makes no difference to me. It will drive the same." Her voice was low and even, but Sarah was shaken. She hadn't been enrolled in car insurance for the past decade. Her license and plates were out of date—her registration sticker was an easy counterfeit. She always bought her vehicles from owners looking to sell, typically old beaters with just enough life in them to get her to work and back. She was of course skirting the law. Her sweat stung the uneasy air.

She realized that the young woman was talking again.

Jo kept trying. "I can pay you cash for the repairs," she offered, "If it's a lot, we could do installments. If you give me your address, I can send you a check each month until it's paid." She toed the concrete floor with the edge of her boot, as if there was a spot she could rub out.

Sarah's eyes finally moved to Jo's. "Not necessary."

"That is too generous of you, Sarah. I really can pay you back. I feel terrible. I don't know what I was thinking. Please, let me take you out for a drink as an apology. Beckman's is just across the street, with some pretty good beers on tap, at least from what I've seen on the sign out front. Please, I feel so bad." Jo's voice was louder now, laced with a quiver that made Sarah intensely uncomfortable.

She calculated the risk. A simple walk and a drink? It was part of the social contract, an olive branch. Something not unenjoyable. It would be enough to make this young woman go away and just keep a small incident what it was—a small incident. Sarah felt her years of running, heavy inside of her, a fatigue down to the marrow. She was tired of her own constant evasion, even when she couldn't always control it. Jo, gawky, sensitive, so young, didn't seem that she could do harm to anyone.

Still, Sarah surprised herself when heard her own voice say, "I can do that."

Jo checked with Tonya, then hurried to gather up her things. Sarah thrust her hands into the pockets of her jeans while she waited. Walking over to Beckman's Pub and Restaurant, the two women looked as unlike friends as it was possible to look. The sun was just starting to set and plenty of people were out and about on the Duluth sidewalks—couples holding hands, parents with strollers, teenagers in all black, lots of dogs. The warm weather drew them out. Some still wore light jackets, others had finally shed them.

Jo berated herself aloud most of the way as she and Sarah made their way toward the pub, then made an effort to point out the ornate wooden sign swinging above the awning of the building. Sarah continued to say nothing, even after they had entered the place and were seated on black leather stools at the very end of the packed bar. The design of the room was dark but luminous—hunter green walls and warm yellow string lights reflected in tiny circles on the deep glossy mahogany of the bar counter. An ancient moose head with fur worn off along the nose was mounted in the far corner. The bartenders popped bottles with bronze openers shaped like antlers. Both women took menus and started reading methodically in silent tandem. The room was loud. Jo kept almost starting to say something. Sarah breathed fast, simply trying to manage herself amidst the sudden clinking and rushing sounds, the laughter, and the closeness of so many bodies. Jo dug her keys out of her pocket and set them on the counter next to her napkin. She flagged the bartender. Sarah stared at the light that caught on the tiny silver star of Jo's keychain.

The stout bartender, his straw-colored hair pulled back in a ponytail, greeted them with a wide smile. "Here you are, ladies!" he said, sliding two filled glasses of beer over, "Our White Wolf IPA."

"Oh," said Jo, eyes wide and concerned. "These aren't ours. We haven't ordered yet." She started to slide hers back toward him.

"Ah, but didn't you see the sign?" he said, "Tall White Wolves on the house for all ladies the whole night tonight. That's you, right? You're in luck—we just got started. Grand opening weekend for our new renovation. Good timing!" His wide smile got even wider. He gestured to a giant chalkboard with pink lettering above the bar that detailed the special event. A group at the center of the bar started cheering about something happening on the TV screens.

"Oh," Jo said again. She looked over at Sarah, who had already taken her first mouthful. Jo followed suit. The frothy draught went down tangy and thick. It was a good taste. The bartender shuffled down the bar to make small talk with some young men wearing fishing vests. Jo smiled at

Sarah and pointed to the glass. "Since this is free, I guess I'll have to get you something off the wine list to thank you, then."

Sarah's face twitched while she pretended to read through the wine selections. The first half of her beer glass was empty within minutes. The warm rush of alcohol in her bloodstream was something she rarely experienced, only now and again when she'd steal into some dive near closing time, when everyone was already intimately involved with their glasses, oblivious to their surroundings. Those were the nights when she worked hardest at forgetting. Now, drinking thirstily in the center of this crowd, it felt like she was swallowing the words she might otherwise have to say, the words she couldn't craft. Her baseline of nervy, electric fear seemed to plane and spread gently down, like a quilt, with every swallow. The murmur of voices enveloped her. She felt like she was shrinking, but that she had decided to do so—a controlled experiment.

"Sarah?" The tousle of Jo's dark hair amplified the worried wrinkle of her forehead. For the first time that day, Sarah let her eyes stop and stay. She looked at Jo. Her feelings softened at Jo's shadowy eyes. The jovial bartender pushed another tall glass her way. She drank deeply, and allowed herself to talk to this young woman, this other person, fellow earth traveler. It felt like she was inhabited by someone else for a moment. Someone free. Someone ordinary.

"I'm sorry," Sarah said. "I am having—there have been unexpected aspects of this day."

Jo bit her lip. "I understand. I know it's my fault. I'm so sorry. I'm trying to get settled in here—I'm actually from, uh, Iowa." She tipped her own glass back. It was clear that she was more than willing to keep pace with Sarah. Drinking looked comfortable and easy on her.

"I'm not native here, either. I understand feeling out of place. I nearly always feel out of place." Sarah coughed, and Jo nodded.

"We have something in common, then."

"Yes."

Jo traced her finger in a wide circle on the smooth wood of the bar.

She glanced at Sarah's bare hands. "Married? Kids?"

"No."

"I don't either. I mean, not married. Not anymore. We'll be signing the final papers soon." Something thick-sounding condensed in Jo's voice. "But to be honest," she said, "I fucking hate talking about it." Sarah smiled at the surprise of Jo's profanity, a real smile, a smile that recognized hollowness. She sighed. This girl suddenly seemed so lost. The wall of sound from the bustling of bar goers surrounded the two of them like a cocoon. Other than the occasional quick brushing-by of someone on their way to the restroom, they were unnoticed—it was as if the last two barstools were somehow secreted away, in the last bar at the edge of the world. It felt remote. Loud. Safe.

"Tell me all the stuff you know about plants," Jo burst out, slapping her hand on the counter. And Sarah did. She told the warmth of the room, she told the bright glare of Jo's eyes, and she told the glasses that appeared in front of her. She told Jo everything she could think of— plants and their growing, their colors, their genetics, their harvest, their propagation. In her words was an arch of imagined foliage that, in another time and place, might have felt to Sarah like the shelter of friendship, maybe even motherhood. Their talk flowed, crested, and ebbed. Jo opened her wallet and added an expensive port to Sarah's queue of glasses. Sarah started to realize that she couldn't keep track of what they were talking about anymore. The dark red slid down, and the conversation lulled, both women starting to let their faces go slack, their eyes glassy. Even through the dulling fog of drink, the lure of home began to play in Sarah's hands like a pinprick, and she mumbled her thanks and waved off, leaving Jo inside and crossing the street to Trenton's parking lot. Her vehicle was there, just as dented and scraped up as when she'd left it.

As Sarah's driving leaned and wove the thirty miles north up the Superior Coast, she realized that she very well might put another dent in the station wagon before she reached her driveway. Mercifully, the roads were dark, dry, and empty.

18

JO STAYED AT THE BAR for one last drink—a Jack with lemon and water to finish the night off right before she settled up. Right there, riding the edge of her limit, it was like drinking stars. She thought about how easily Sarah had downed a good amount of alcohol, and in just a couple short hours. It always annoyed Jo that people assumed women couldn't drink like men. They could. And they did. Sarah seemed completely fine when she left.

The glass of whiskey was placed on a fresh black napkin square. Jo took her first gulp right away. It was best when the ice was whole and fresh. She couldn't stop replaying the moment of impact with Sarah's car in her head. She'd gotten herself into such stupid trouble so soon into her new job. It was remarkable, she thought, how quickly and soundly she could fuck up—she laughed to herself about that one. So many ventures she attempted ended up so pathetically bound straight for the seafloor. Adjusting well at the new job? Go ahead and crash a cart full of metal into a consultant's car. Getting married to your hometown sweetheart? Don't bother about details of compatibility. Need to distance yourself from your problems and start over in a new city? Well, getting wasted was what she seemed to be doing right now. Her life was there in the whiskey glass, going down, down.

Jo started to wonder if she'd overdone it. The room was swimming.

Standing up to leave seemed difficult. The man who had taken Sarah's spot on the stool next to Jo started talking spiritedly about nuclear power, something she knew nothing about. She smiled placidly at him but shook herself back to an imitation of sobriety when she found his hand around her waist and felt his cigarette-scented stubble brush her neck. She drifted left to stand in a different corner until her card came back from the bartender. She could still smell the man with the roaming hands on her skin. Scrolling through the too-bright screen of her phone, she thought of texting Cait to see if she could come pick her up. But Cait had done that enough when they were college kids. Jo was supposed to be past that. She found her cab service app and reserved a driver instead. Once the ride was confirmed, Jo clutched her purse and tottered up to the pub hostess, holding her head. The woman shot her a reproachful, *oh, honey* kind of smile. Jo sat down in a booth near the entryway to sway a little until the driver came. Waste of a fare. She hadn't counted her remaining cash, but she knew there couldn't be much left.

The car ride was quiet as Jo concentrated on sitting up straight and grasping the door handle with her right hand. In a matter of minutes, she was in front of her apartment building. She thrust a ten-dollar bill into the waiting hand of the driver and mumbled her thanks. She nodded to one of her neighbors who was leaving the building and held the door open for her. She watched the steps carefully, focusing on looking like she had full control of her faculties. Her feet scuffed as she made her dizzy way through the hallway to her apartment door.

An important thought speared up through the haze. *Keys.* Even as Jo clawed through her purse and pockets, she knew. She'd left them on the counter at the bar. She had no way to get inside.

Summoning the concentration to squint at her phone, she found the number for Beckman's Pub and dialed. The pleasant hostess answered and reassured her that the keys were found and would be held for her at the hosting station up front. Then she asked, "Are you the one with the short hair who just left?"

"Yeah," Jo said weakly, and hung up. That left her standing feebly in front of her door, head still reeling, and no cash left. She would have to walk the six blocks back to pick up her keys, drunk, in the dark. Her stomach turned at the thought. Leaning against her door, she slumped to the stain-worn carpet of the hallway floor. No one was around. She let herself close her eyes just for a moment, wondering what she was doing with her life.

Her phone started vibrating in pairs of long tones. "I'm not home," she said aloud. Whoever her caller was did not want to talk to her right now. She felt too alone to talk. She found herself wishing she could send out a beam to make everyone in the world feel alone. She knew how pathetic it all was. Six blocks was a long walk right now. She reached up to try the doorknob again—maybe it was somehow unlocked? But no. God, she thought, she'd definitely had too much. She turned about on her knees and punched the door with the heel of her hand. She moaned. She hammered on the door three more times with all her strength. Then, she started to sob right there in the middle of the hallway, because she could no longer care enough not to, until something stunned her to silence.

The door opened.

It was then that she surmised that she was not in front of the door to unit 15 after all. She was crying in a heap in front of unit 13, and whoever it was who lived there.

A silhouette of a man looked down at the messy spill of a woman, through the small gap that his still-fastened chain lock allowed. He was cast in darkness, features impossible to make out. "Hi," he said, his voice clear as a chime. "Look, I think you have the wrong door."

When she didn't respond other than just staring up at him, he cleared his throat and pointed to the right. "Aren't you in number fifteen?"

19

HOWARD HAD BEEN GETTING READY for bed, putting fresh sheets on his mattress and thinking about starting to run the water to heat up for his evening shower, when he heard a woman's distressed voice and the jiggle of an attempt to open his door. Through the peephole, he caught close glimpses of her odd unraveling. He was fairly sure she was the neighbor from across the hall. He had no intention of intervening until she started getting agitated.

She didn't look right. It was definitely his neighbor. She did not look well. A rush of concern swept over him. He watched her movements through the peephole. She seemed sluggish, and very badly inebriated.

Maybe she was confused, thinking she couldn't unlock what she thought was her apartment. He decided to open the door, just a crack, enough to quietly redirect her, praying that she'd simply stumble across to her own door and get herself to bed.

He hurried to the pile of cosmetics on the kitchen table to check his face in the compact mirror. He smeared over a spot of foundation that had smudged off earlier in the day, probably some absentminded touch of his wrist. The color went wetly over his cheekbone. The woman sounded like she was crying outside the door. Considering the state she was in, he guessed it was unlikely she'd notice nuances in his facial appearance. It was dark enough. She was gone enough. He hoped she would just mumble a sloppy apology and shuffle off. But the sooner the crying stopped, the better.

Howard flicked off the closest lamp and opened the door, just a few inches, chain lock still on. To her, looking in, his apartment would be nothing but a dark column, barely lit by a faint glow, the single light of the kitchen, the dimmer slid all the way down. Howard, backlit and even darker, was just barely visible, the shape of a man on the edge of the shadows with a gentle voice.

"Aren't you in number fifteen?" he asked, but she stayed right where she was, leaning against his doorframe, glaring up at him as if he'd said something far more offensive.

"I left my keys at the bar," she said, too loud. "I can't get into my apartment. I need to go get them. But I can't right now. Look, I had a little too much and I need to just take a minute." To Howard's horror, she started yelling, directing all the sound she could summon straight at the half of Howard's face that peered down through the gap of the open door. "You know what? *Don't* tell me which door is *mine*! Do I look *stupid* to you? I'm trying to handle things!" She managed to get her feet underneath her and draw herself up, but the strap of her purse got lodged beneath the door where Howard had opened it. She tugged at it, furious. It was stuck fast, the leather folded sideways between the door and seal. Three more swift yanks to no result, and the young woman sank to the floor again in puffy-eyed agony.

Howard heard another neighbor's rustlings. Soon, a second door opened further down the hall. A woman in a grubby robe with her hair wrapped up on top of her head looked ready to eviscerate someone. "Hey!" she yelled, index finger rigid and fist clenched. "It is almost ten o'clock at night. Some of us have work in the morning. We're calling the cops if you can't wrap it up down there." She punctuated her sentiment with a slam.

Shit, thought Howard. He imagined how this exchange must look, happening in front of his door. A domestic dispute. He was embarrassed and, worse, now too far into the situation. Officers at his door were not a complication he could accept. They would have questions. They would want a good, hard look at his face. "Sh, hey." Howard rushed to unclasp his chain lock and swung the door all the way open, freeing the purse. His shadow bent to Jo, raised her to her feet with his palms beneath her elbows, and guided her inside the apartment, his heart pounding wildly.

"Here," he said, helping her sit down on the wooden bench in his entryway. "It's OK, all right?" He reached out a hand but stopped short of touching her. She sat straight up and clutched the purse. He noticed her forearms shaking.

"I need to get my keys," she said, slowly, more to herself than to him. "I need to get inside, and I need to feed my cat." A tear slid silently out of her left eye.

Howard cleared his throat. So that was all? "Uh, listen—if you want, I think I have the number of the night-shift maintenance guy. I'm sure he has a master key and could get you into your place."

"Really?" Her face had sharp facets, like a gemstone. The dim light glanced off her right cheek and eyebrow, the other side still dark.

"Yes," Howard said. A small smile. He tugged downward at his sleeves. She couldn't be able to see anything strange about his face in the darkness—there was no way. He recited that reassurance in his mind as he strove for a casual tone. "I'm pretty sure the landlord keeps him on staff in case somebody's toilet starts flooding or something." Howard ducked around the corner and into the kitchen, leaving his neighbor to collect herself. A list of important phone numbers was neatly taped to the inside of his leftmost cabinet door. He could see in the dim light just enough to copy the number down on an index card. He handed it to Jo with "PM Emergency Maintenance" written in his even handwriting next to the number. Her phone was already out, and she started dialing immediately. Howard retreated to the kitchen again. He paced quietly while she called. The wall of the short foyer blocked him from her view.

The volume on Jo's phone was turned up loud enough that Howard clearly heard the twelve rings, and then the gruff but well-meaning voice that agreed to be down to help in about fifteen minutes, just outside Jo's door.

That meant that Howard had another fifteen minutes alone with his neighbor, whom he might never talk to again. He couldn't think of one thing to say. But she was walking over to the table, to him, in the almost dark.

"Could I use your bathroom?"

He nodded and pointed around the corner, though she had already found her way. She must have the same layout in her place, he thought, turning away from the bright fluorescence as she flicked on the bathroom light. He tried not to listen to the rustling and trickling audible through the door. Howard felt strange having her enter that same space where his body first shattered to red, where his cheek had rested in terror on the cold tile of the floor. He suddenly worried for her. There could be some energy, some entity remaining to send her mind floating above a frozen lake reflecting cold moonlight, incarnating some long-held fear, turning to her own wraith because she had unknowingly entered the shadow of his.

As it was, she came out just the same as she had gone in. But she left the light on. It beamed a thick yellow line onto the uneven linoleum of the kitchen floor.

"Why is your mirror covered up?" she asked.

"Oh," he said, faltering, his mind racing for something plausible. "I'm having the bathroom paint updated soon—figured I'd protect the glass."

"Oh. I just painted, too! My bedroom, though," said Jo. "Hey, I think I wrote you a note on a package outside your door a couple days ago? It was left at my door at first." She came over and sat beside him. She moved the chair closer to him and put her elbows on the table, hands clutching her head through rumpled black hair.

"Really?" he said, tipping his chin down, brushing his almond hair down over his eyebrows. "I guess it must have been mine. I didn't see the note, sorry."

She tilted her head at him. The light from the kitchen chandelier, even low as it was, filtered through three slivers of reddish translucence on his face where the makeup had been hastily smeared. A glow bounced through the delicate inside lining of his eyelids. Howard held still. Jo was watching his face like it was a goddamn sunset. He couldn't breathe.

"Your face . . . it looks—? It looks really cool in this light. It's almost glowing or something." He scrambled for something to say, another cover—he should have rehearsed this already. He had nothing. But even as his lips parted in silence, she was standing up, walking into the little living room. Howard heard his own heart. He took in a silent, shaky breath to ease his nerves. He darted a glance at the clock. Ten more minutes.

Jo ran her hand along the lower shelf of the skinny walnut hutch where Howard stored what he thought of as his miscellanea. The bottled ships, interesting rocks, that kind of thing. On the top shelf, which Jo gasped at, was a small collection of old cameras that Howard occasionally added to, a carryover interest from his undergraduate days as a journalism student. "Wow, these are wonderful," she said, "Do you mind if I look at them?" Even despite her unsteady hands, Howard nodded a go-ahead before he had a chance to think. She stretched her thin arm up toward the white Polaroid Spectra and its accompanying stack of film in packs with shiny metallic wrapping. She took the camera off the shelf and slid the big button on the side, popping open the dusty casing. The lens inside gleamed, clean and purple black. Howard had never actually opened the camera up. "You know how to load it, right?" she asked, pulling the first package of film from the shelf.

"No," said Howard. She made a small sound of disbelief. He smiled. "I like the way they look, but I don't really know how to use most of them. I got that one last year, on eBay. It's fully functional, refurbished and everything. I think the film is the new stuff that Polaroid makes—it came with it." He was surprised how easily the words came to him. He felt easy with her, talking about such a fantastic object. Howard loved the elegance of the old machines, the feel of the bulky casing, a kind of stateliness that they communicated. In her hands, though, the old Spectra looked practically joyful.

"My grandpa had one of these," she said, clicking open the loading door and peering inside. She blew a quick puff of air to clear out any dust. "He used to take us on picnics when we came to visit, when I was little, and he would let me take one picture on his Polaroid each time, just one. He got to take the rest, you know, of me and my mom wearing matching sunglasses or just shots of trees or the docks, kids jumping into the lake." She peeled open the film wrapping and loaded a cartridge as she talked. Her fingers flipped deftly. "It was such magic, that there was nothing on the paper, just that muddy shiny color and then the image came through . . . like we were preserved, just perfect, just there, forever. I still have a bunch of them in a shoebox somewhere, and my grandpa's camera. I still have it. I'll have to show you sometime." She clacked the film loading door shut, and it automatically spit forth the protective film sheet into Jo's expectant palm. The indicator light glowed green. She posed dramatically, the camera hoisted against her hip. "We always said that everything is picturesque on Polaroid." She smirked. Then she asked, "Do you want to see how it works?" Her eyes were warm, wet.

"Sure," he said. He wanted her to put a blanket around his shoulders. He wanted to sing for her. He wanted her to open all the cameras on the shelf—anything. The minutes were slipping by.

Standing beside him, she quickly pointed to the different buttons. She showed him how to hold it, frame his shot, and click the shutter. "One thing, though," she said, "We'll definitely need more light. These old cameras don't really do well in this low indoor light. Even if that flash still works, it's not much. Here." She flew to crank up the dimmer in the kitchen and switch on two more lamps. Howard froze, failing to think of a reason to say why she shouldn't. He jerked the camera up to block his face, and breathed, looking at his apartment through the viewfinder, feeling dizzy, removed. Panning left, he found his neighbor giving him a soft expression, her hand lifted in a wave. Howard took the shot. The mechanical advance of the Polaroid out of the front of the camera synchronized with the buzz of Jo's phone—the maintenance worker was outside, waiting to let her in. Howard put the developing photo on the table and swiftly turned off the lamp nearest to him.

"Looks like I'd better go," she said. "Thanks for taking me in. My name is Jo. I'm not always such a disaster." She extended her hand, which he took lightly in his. She laughed. His other hand still held the camera, partially obscuring his face from her.

"Howard," he said, his left eye peeking at her.

She laughed. "OK, Howard. See you 'round. Sorry about all this. God. Wait—your name is Howard? Are you the one selling the truck that's out back? I sent you an email. I want to buy it."

"Oh, ah—yeah. That is me. I'll have to look for your message."

She nodded excitedly. "OK! OK, thanks. 'Night!"

She closed the door behind her. He walked back to the kitchen table, wiping his forehead with the back of his hand. As he saw the color that came away, he realized that he'd been sweating. He felt the room settle back into its normal order, just the space, and him alone in the middle of it.

The square Polaroid photograph sat on the table, still developing from sketched suggestion into color. He sat patiently, and when it came almost fully clear, he picked up the picture, careful to only touch the very edges. Jo's figure emerged then—hair amok, hip jutted a bit to the left, hand poised in a delicate wave, and a face that caught the light in a strange way, whetted and keen.

Drifting through the cold, black water, the fish contracted and expanded his thick cords of muscle, monstrous head weaving side to side as the powerful tail pumped along. The way, even in underwater blackness, shone within his fish memory like moonlit trails traced on the backside of his eyes. He may live for fifty years, and yet his joining along this path was young compared to the hundreds of millions of years marking the history of his kin. Their shadows swam beneath him, burrowed into the fossil record, powdered into inoffensive sand. The whisper of their milt now swirled in his blood, a legacy of anatomical schematics already perfected in an age past.

The fish moved without flaw—engineered that way by nature, by the winds propelling the waves of this lake, by depths untold, by the sense of water flowing from safe shallows. The reeds and rocks felt his passage before he approached. He was a creature incapable of fear, ancient enough to be sure of his strong heart. He drove forward. Small whirls of water spun behind him.

Part Two

20

SARAH WOKE UP TO THE swishing brush-tap of new aspen leaves that the heavy morning wind moved against her bedroom window. The strong pine frame of the cabin would hold her safe if a storm was coming, she thought. It had done so many times. But something wasn't right. Her ears rang as she sat up in bed. She remembered the harrowing drive home from the night before. She felt ill. Sarah ran her thumbs over her eyebrows. She pressed her fingers into twin pressure points on her forehead and tried to think, but whispers in her brain deafened the ability to sort her senses.

She remembered the girl from the floral shop damaging her car. She didn't care about that one way or the other as long as the vehicle still ran—the station wagon was a relic. It had come along with the little cabin when she bought it. She'd paid in cash for both, to a bearded man who was Canada-bound and didn't want any questions. The car was fine. A dent hardly mattered.

But the girl, Jo, had been devastated over it. And then they had ended up at that blaring pub with its bartenders and the amber sludge that she'd taken in like an IV. Her head pounded. She reached for the collection of pill bottles at her bedside and dry swallowed her strongest painkiller. She swung her legs over the bed, bare feet touching the cool, rough wooden planks of the floor. An oily film clung to her thoughts of last night. Had she said anything to compromise herself? She was sure that she'd talked about plants for the most part. But she remembered Jo asking for her address, something about sending her payments to fix the car. She would never have given out her address—hers wasn't even a real address. One Superior Road was just what she filled out when she couldn't avoid a form. Her driveway was dirt. GPS didn't lead anyone here accurately. The only people she ever saw around were hikers, in backpacks, pocketed pants, wide hats, and fluorescent shirts. They occasionally wandered off the overgrown path that led down to a very small waterfall, Moss Falls. It was a half mile south of the cabin.

Moss Falls. Had she told Jo about Moss Falls? Sarah thought she remembered there being a question about places to hike. No. Places to photograph. Jo asked her. Had she answered? She couldn't remember exactly what she had said, but the thought of Moss Falls set off a quivering sense of error in her head.

Stop, she told herself. It was nothing. But still the paranoia welled. In her memory of Jo's drunken goodbye, Sarah now recalled, or maybe replaced, a knowing glance. Maybe Jo suspected Sarah's real identity, recognized her from an old missing-person bulletin. Maybe she'd report her, out of a perceived kindness. It wasn't impossible, and that was enough of a fissure for plausibility to seep through. Sarah rose and walked to the kitchen. She pulled the knob for cold water and scrubbed her face icy and raw. The fear was like an itch, deep beneath the skin, that couldn't be eased with anything other than the absolute quiet of true safety. The tapping of the aspen leaves against the window sounded like fingers now.

Sarah looked back toward the bedroom. No one. For a moment, she felt she was back at the university, thought she heard the wheels of a gurney against a cool floor. In the next second, her mind leapt desperately, outstretched, toward the part of her that soothed toward the reasonable. But she couldn't make the jump against the opposing force. It was a rolling wave without a shore.

Leave now.

Leave now.

Leave now.

Haphazard curtains of light hair swinging, she ran outside, around the back of the house to the loose pile of old boards that lay beneath a great black spruce. She hauled trios of half-rotted planks back to the house, dragging them through the tall, stinging grass. The wind spun her hair into a tangle. She moved both her hands in front of her face, clutching them to the bridge of her nose in a gesture like prayer. She nearly bent in half, but then straightened instead, lifting the blond snare away from her eyes. Hair snagged in her hands.

Back inside, she yanked on one of the kitchen drawers so hard that it came free past the catch and clattered to the floor. In the spill of the drawer's contents, her fingers sought a box of nails—some new, some rusted and bent but carefully replaced. Leaving the mess on the floor, she rushed to find the toolbox that held her heavy framing hammer.

The sounds of the wind were joined by the rapid warning cries of an osprey that alighted on the peak of the cabin's gable roof. Then the bird flew off, leaving behind only the even thudding sounds of Sarah's hammer as she began to board up the windows.

21

HOWARD ROSE WHEN IT WAS still dark, finally frustrated enough to abandon his bed. His attempts to sleep grew more fruitless the more he longed for it. A shivering restlessness had arrived inside him, and it would not quiet.

He couldn't shake the hot cling of the damp sheets around him, even as he got up to move, head reeling, to his writing desk. His face felt heavy. He opened his laptop, searching for something to watch or work on. In the dark, the glow of the screen shone up through the red of Howard's chin, casting shadows of teeth through his cheeks from inside. It created a faint pink halo at the bottom of his vision as his blood flowed, illuminated, beneath his lower eyelids. His veins felt charged. His blood spun up, fluttery.

He sorted through the freelance leads he had bookmarked. Lately, he was getting good at channeling everything he had into his work. It was a constant that grounded him. His productivity as a writer was surging in a way it never had. As he clicked open a request from a client and started taking down some notes about how he'd approach the project, his bleary sleepless brain dropped everything else it was holding to streamline the task. Bullet points moved into paragraphs. The right words were coming fast, and Howard's veined, glassy fingers flew to keep up. But even that frantic tapping of hands barely staved off whatever it was that drove him forward, whatever was happening, still, inside of him.

The morning crept through the shades while Howard spent the sunrise lost in words, pretending to speak as his client aloud here and there to test the sound. He went back, changing the arc of his phrasing, adding power with words inserted or taken away. He cut a paragraph, taking the best line of it and moving it to the middle of another. He considered the tone of his commentary, substituting words until the voice was right. He was in a trance of keystrokes, and through it he could see the shape of the finished piece coming together. Another article nearly done, and in one sitting. He held his forehead in his palm.

The month's rent was easily covered with the money from his recent product reviews. With this story and the shipwreck piece, he had a good start on next month, too. Maybe this would be the year that he could send one of his mother's checks back to her uncashed, with a message that she didn't need to support him anymore, that she should focus on living her own life. The curse on his body, he thought, was also like a sharpening. Maybe it was helping him.

He was rethinking the words of the article's final line when he heard the faint click of the door from apartment 15 being opened and shut. Blood thumped in his head as he rushed to his own door in ten quick strides. He pressed his eye to the peephole. There she was.

Jo held a knuckle to her forehead for a moment, then reached into her purse for her absent keys. After a slight hesitation, she nodded to herself, reopened the door, reached around the doorknob, and locked it from the inside, blocking the escape of an inquisitive, tail-up cat with her foot. She was wearing an oversized cable-knit sweater, royal blue. Howard realized he was smiling. He felt drawn to her. He wondered if she'd slept well.

She turned to walk away, but then stopped and looked directly at Howard—or, rather, his apartment door. To his surprise, rather than walking out down the hallway, she stepped to the front of his door, and his view through the peephole quickly became a fuzzily cropped close-up of his neighbor's cheekbone and forehead. Suddenly his voyeurism humiliated him. He closed his eyes, but stayed at the door, breathing as quietly as he could. He didn't see Jo as she pressed her hand to the door, smoothed a bit of tape that fixed a note, and bit her lip in a moment of wordless apology. He only heard her walk away. When he opened his eyes again, her footfalls had faded to silence.

He wasn't sure how long he stood at the door. He felt so tired and still, staring at the now-empty circular frame of the peephole. He drank in the deep green of the door's surface until his vision blurred.

This time, he felt it coming on. His thoughts split. His senses erred. He braced his hands against the door, and the room fell away.

He stood in silent snowfall. Before him was a field of blinding white bordered by trees. Their branches sagged under the burden of snow. The wind stung his cheeks, and the sky shone with cold. Crystalline planes of ice scattered the landscape. The warring clack of antlers sounded in the distance. He could feel the weight of his body pressing his feet to the chilled ground.

Lightheaded, Howard stumbled backward, trying to shut his eyes against the searing hallucination, but his sheer eyelids hardly veiled his vision. A sense of terror seized him as the field faded to black, snow still falling even in a void of darkness. When the reality of his apartment finally came back into view, he clambered toward his bed and felt despair settle like a stone in a bucket. He twisted the sheets in his hands. A fever-ish union of hot and cold blood enveloped him. Unable to comprehend his body, afraid to trust his mind, he was profoundly alone.

Howard breathed in slowly, filling his lungs as deep as he could. There seemed no end to it. The empty space inside him had become cav-ernous. He thought of Jo, the shape of her waist. He thought of the way the wintering earth opened to him in his vision, calling to him in a way that both bound him in fear and laced him with need.

He wanted to be able to see the sky. The real sky.

He wanted to be touched. His body surged like a current in a faulty twist of shorted wire. But he was a monster in the shadows. His want had nowhere to go.

Pressure hurtled through his veins. What more? he wondered, breathing through a strange ache that radiated through his torso. He sank to his knees, then rolled onto his back. He could feel the back of his skull, solid against the floor. Searching for something to ground him, he traced the lines of the fine ceiling cracks with his eyes. The pain was charged, whirring. In the madness of it, he pressed his hands together as hard as he could, until the muscles of his arms shook. A slight relief. The pressure seemed to release something.

He started a set of sit-ups. His core wrenched up, flinging his hair forward with each rep. The movement stilled the pain, and he dug into it, raising his shoulders up from the floor again and again, contracting and releasing his abdominals in a relentless pulse. He went until his fatigue was electric. It was like a story he was telling his body. He almost couldn't stop, but when he did, he could barely stand. His back was slick with sweat. He needed air.

He lifted the window open. The cool smell of morning air rushed in. He pulled his shirt off and used it to wipe the wet mess from his face, thick streaks of makeup coming away on the fabric. He pressed his nose to the screen, breathing in hungrily. He listened for the waves in the distance, but the wind wasn't coming from the right direction. The air was sweet though, like spring water, and the way he could taste it overcame him. He rolled his shoulders backwards and fought to relax, in all his power and all his fragility. In the street below, he watched a few birds flutter from tree to tree. He heard happy shrieks of children laughing somewhere on the block. The musculature of his back, deep in its red, announced itself in the way it curved and sighed on either side of his spine, around his shoulder blades. Reds and darker reds.

Looking down at his arm, Howard squeezed his fist and watched things move. He asked himself what it meant to be hopeless. He asked himself if he could stay in his apartment for another week without becoming so. He could feel things outside the window. What did it mean to want? And what was that wanting? It would have been simple enough to long for a lover, but it wasn't that, not truly. His interest in Jo, of course, had begun shading into something like imagining her hand at his hip, her mouth finding his, feeling whole beneath her. But those thoughts were sketches of a much older stirring he felt. It wasn't like something calling him, no—it was like everything was calling him, his bones themselves the receivers of a scrambled transmission, his skin the response to a question formed in wilder places, where he had never learned the grammar.

Howard heaved out a slow breath. The late morning sun worked its way further into the sky.

22

JO DOUBLE-CHECKED HER TEXT MESSAGES to see if she had found the right place. The address matched, even though it appeared she was standing by the side of a warehouse. Cait had mentioned in her messages last night that the entrance would look a little strange, but that she'd know she was in the right place once she was inside. Cait's excitement about Jo's plan to finally get to the trails bubbled over through the chat box. "There's no point in living near the North Shore if you're never going to put on your hiking boots," Cait had written. Never mind that Jo's hiking boots were just boots. Never intended for rugged terrain. She didn't mention that to Cait. It didn't matter. She could walk in them just fine.

So many things pointed Jo toward the North Woods. Cait kept telling her to get out into nature, that it would make her feel better. And Sarah lived up that way, too. Jo's pride nagged like a papercut to get Sarah some money for the car repair. And on top of that, holding the camera in Howard's apartment the other night reminded her how much she missed taking photos. Her prized Nikon DSLR sat, probably collecting its first layer of dust by now, in a box under her bed. She reminded herself to charge the battery. She hadn't shot at all since signing the first divorce papers. As far as anyone would be able to tell, it had never been used—the camera's memory had zero images on it. Nothing but black. She'd deleted all the saved images back in Iowa. So many of them had been of Joshua, catching him laughing or concentrating or fixing something at the house. He never looked straight at the lens but turned away. It always infuriated her, but she learned to steal shots of him candidly. She destroyed that proof of their life together, as if that could've made it not exist. All the photos of Joshua, and then all the photos of anyone, until just vistas and still lifes remained. But even as she scrolled through those photos, she felt like she could sense him in them, too, just outside the frame. She remembered clicking through, five hundred and twenty times, watching each thumbnail disappear as she hit delete, delete, delete, delete. She remembered how close she came to pitching the empty camera to the floor lens-first afterward, but she loved it too much. Instead, she wrapped it in an old T-shirt and put it with the meager pile of things she could bear to take with her when she moved out.

As Jo shook her thoughts away and approached the outfitter, she saw the sign with the crossed paddle logo. She went inside and entered a world of flannel, durable plastic, and woodsmoke. The aisles were packed tight with outdoor gear of all kinds, from coolers to camp stoves. Cait had sent her to the right place, of course. Jo watched the customers, most of them dressed in simple clothes that looked waterproof and were worn in easy angles on their athletic bodies. Jo rearranged her own shirt at the neckline.

Maybe she could be someone like that, she thought. Maybe she could become one of these quietly inscrutable people, looking thoughtfully at a green thermos with brows knit, clipping and unclipping the straps of rucksacks in different configurations, tugging briskly at a jacket sleeve to check its durability. The store ceiling was low, and the light was dim. It felt cozy and lodge-like. A fire crackled in the wood fireplace near the main entrance at the front of the store. A woman in a loose white shirt glanced at her as she passed. Jo looked up and away, absentmindedly blotting her lipstick off with the back of her hand. She studied the shadows on the ceiling at first, but then saw something suspended from above with strong orange cords. Her eyes drank in the hue of a long cedar strip canoe with its brilliant natural wood grain showing through beneath the finish.

Jo reached up to brush a finger against the bottom of the boat, but she couldn't quite reach. It was gorgeous. She imagined heaving a pack and a hiking pole into the canoe's belly, pushing off from a dock, her paddle pulling sure and strong against clear vast water with sheer cliffs towering above her along the shore. The sun would glance off the rocks, and she would sip icy water from a canteen. A loon would cry against the quiet. Trees would rise from the shoreline, creating a corridor, leading her along beneath the sky.

Maybe someone else would be sitting on the back seat, watching the strength of her bare shoulders in the sun, offering his own strokes, propelling them further into open channels of pristine wilderness. Jo shut her eyes.

"Are you interested?" said a sandy voice behind her. She turned and saw a gangly young man with a name tag pinned to his polo. He pointed up. "I could bring her down for you."

"Oh, no . . . no. Just daydreaming." She noticed a huge painting of a gray wolf on the wall behind her. She loved that, too. She wanted to touch everything in the store, even though she was pretty sure she could afford none of it.

"Hey, I get it," said the guy with the name tag, gesturing upward at the canoe. It's a work of art. Way better than the old beat-up green Wenonah I've got in my shed." He put one hand in his back pocket. "Anything else I can help you find?"

"I'm actually just looking for some maps of the area, hiking trails, things like that."

"Oh, sure! Head right on up front and talk to my brother," he said, pointing the way to someone on the other side of the store. Jo saw the resemblance. He yelled out, "Paul! This customer's looking for hiking maps!" Paul waved her over. He showed her a selection of laminated trifolds for Gooseberry Falls and Tettegouche State Park. She flipped through the options, skimmed through names of roads and trailheads. She picked out three to take. Paul also grabbed a piece of paper off a lopsided stack tucked behind the glossy map display. It looked like a photocopy of something drawn by hand.

"This one is free," he said, pointing at the center of the paper as he slid it over the counter in front of her. "The best kept secrets, the little spots that you don't hear about. Better for seeing wildlife in the warm season when the bigger parks are overrun." He circled a couple things in pencil, talking about trail quality and geographic features. Waterfalls seemed to be a popular part of the terrain—he named several.

"What about Moss Falls?" she asked. "Is that one of the spots on here?" She scanned the map but didn't see it in the muddle of lines and names.

"Ah, right here," he said, scribbling a new label and circling it three times. "That's a real nice little one. Surprised you've heard of it! Great short hike. Trails are overgrown some, but nothing you can't push through. Just wear your bug repellent."

"Oh, I'll need some of that, too," said Jo. He snatched two bottles from behind the register and dropped them in a canvas bag with the maps. She thanked him. He was so young, but he moved with easy confidence. What must it be like, she wondered, to know wild places well enough to circle them on the map for someone else, to know something by heart that held the edge of fear for others. But now that she had her maps, she wondered what she might begin to know.

On her way out, Jo paused to look at a framed image hanging on the wall near the door. The outline of Lake Superior was traced out in white against a black background. Small boat icons marked the known shipwrecks on the lake since the 1800s, each labeled with its date of sinking. The little ships covered the whole lake. So many, she thought, and walked out the door.

23

WHEN THE LAST BOARD WAS nailed solidly to the last cabin window, Sarah rubbed her thumbs across the wood-splintered pads of her fingers. She took an academic interest in the texture of them, the lack of pain. Nobody could see in or out. The cabin was ready to go dormant, windows secured against vandals or buffeting winds until her return. If there was to be a leaving. If there was to be a return.

She approached the doorless coat closet and lifted out her old green toolbox. Wrapping the hammer neatly in a rag, she tucked it back into the battered Craftsman. She was careful to secure each of the three metal latches on the box. The third veered to the side, refusing to latch until she pressed the side hard into place. She tugged on the toolbox handle to ensure that it wouldn't fly open and spill its sharp metal contents. Then she replaced the toolbox on the shelf, wedged in between a microscope and an accordion file filled with seed specimens in labeled, sealed foil packets. The closet's contents were immaculately cataloged and organized in small stacks and rows. Even as much as Sarah ran, as much as her names, accounts, and addresses rotated, she couldn't fully discard the material weight of her past self. A few pieces of lab and medical equipment were mingled in with the broom and the mop—a box of glass slides, a package of latex gloves, a bag of syringes, fluid bags, continuous feed printouts of lab results—they were things that she kept near to her when she didn't need to stash them in a storage locker during a transition. Their curse was heavy, anchoring them to her. Now, in the strange, creeping light that found her through a crack or two in the hastily nailed wooden planks, Sarah found herself feeling underground. So far below that no one sees, she thought. But something was stretching upward in her mind.

"This is crazy," she whispered aloud. "Why is this happening again? What am I doing?" She kicked a box of files feebly, walked to the kitchen, and lurched out the door. Haggard and confused out in the yard, she shielded her eyes with a palm out to the sun. She felt a brief clearing of sky open beneath her pounding desire to run. Down the hill, glittering light on the river drew her forward. Her stumbling walk smoothed into a purposed stride. She recited the plant life in her head as she passed, with names like the names of children, and she imagined them as such. *Jack Pine. Marsh Vetchling. White Cedar. Mountain Maple. Black Ash. Inland Juneberry. Sand Violet.* The trees of the northern forest, safe and unbent through rain and snow, through whipping winds. She walked. The trees—they were lasting. They were consistent. Sarah's hand brushed the tall grass. She wound her way down. Rocks crunched underfoot as she finally reached the edge of the water at the bottom of the hill. The air, she noticed, was newly warm. The river looked high.

A rush of water parted as a green-black fin broke the surface of the otherwise calm inlet and disappeared again with a swoosh of tail. A sturgeon. Sarah smiled at the surfacing, no doubt a male, since they arrived first—the sturgeon would be spawning soon. Such a fish, she thought. Such unique physiology. An ancient creature in terms of evolutionary history, the sturgeon was coated with bony plates rather than scales and could live over a century. The heart of the creature, she remembered learning, was remarkable and primitive. In embryo, the heart was the first organ to develop, starting to form at the front of the head and undergoing a ninety-degree positional shift as the fish grew, the emerging protective layer around the heart shaped like a little half-moon. The process was slow, compared to that of other fishes. Yet, the sturgeon's heart was, in design, still so similar to those of more modern vertebrates. Evolution was conservative. Two hundred million years would not greatly alter the blueprint. Sarah felt a pang settle on her breathing. She thought about the slow grace of eons and eons of veins and vessels, at play long before anyone thought to study them. Wanting to understand such elegant forces had defined her career as a scientist. But what was she now?

Another huge fish broke the surface. It wouldn't be long now, Sarah thought. Soon, their dance would begin. Another generation born to the river.

She squatted, then sat by the waterside, slow minutes passing one after the next. She watched the wild sedge ripple in the breeze up the hill. She counted the small rock ferns clinging to the low rock face where the river turned, green lichen and hoary moss dappling it like brushstrokes. She stretched out and listened to the water, pillowing her head on her arm. The earth moved in time to the slow prickle of stems and leaves against her neck. Face to the ground, she felt like she could see it anew— small honey-colored pebbles gave way to gray and red as the land sloped down to the riverbed. Another sturgeon popped his nose to the surface. Sarah smiled. When she felt steady, she rose stiffly and climbed the hill back up to the cabin.

She was scheduled to work at Ahlborn's that evening, and she arrived as usual—tidy and unassuming, as if nothing had happened. She spent eight hours absently scanning the cereal of strangers and adhering to pleasantries with vacant eyes, fighting to drown the desire to stride right out the door, box up all her possessions, and run.

24

BY NINE O'CLOCK THE FOLLOWING evening, Howard's limbs were burning. He couldn't focus it away. He couldn't even work on his writing. The ache he had worked away the day before was back, and it was everywhere.

The need for movement overwhelmed every other physical sensation. He counted the days he had been inside his apartment. It had been nearly two weeks now. He struggled to blend his usual layers of pigment onto his face. His skin was becoming much more sensitive—even a slight touch resulted in a sharp stinging. His muscles buzzed with a constant insistence, like they had a will, and were refusing atrophy. It was impossible to be still.

He found some small relief by pacing the short length of the apartment over and over again, his steps unraveling and respooling an endless thread of need. He had to go outside. His body craved it, pulled him toward it like a just-born gravity. Keeping the window open to the air no longer helped—it just made him want to hurl himself out of it. Any action created the need for more, compelled him to bring himself into a wider space. He needed to breathe without being separated from the sky. He needed it. Tonight. Damn the consequences.

He retouched his foundation, even though it stung. He watched the sky deepen from twilight blue to black. He wore long pants and long sleeves, and his black sweatshirt with its hood up to obscure his face. He looked down and stepped across the threshold. He stood up straighter. As he quickly locked his door, he saw a handwritten note taped under the knocker. He plucked the paper from the door, eyes jumping to the signature at the bottom. Jo. He held the paper lightly. It was smooth and thin. Her writing was sure and angular.

> Howard—
>
> Sorry again for the other night. You probably never want to see me again, but I do want to ask about your truck! Is it still for sale? If you're willing to let me test drive, please reply to my email sent last week. (Subject line: Green F250 for sale)
>
> Or you could also knock on my door any time. Thanks . . . for all of it.
>
> Your neighbor,
>
> Jo

Howard folded the note into an uneven square and slid it into his back pocket. Soon, he was walking into the night. He wanted sorely to rub at his face. He winced at the wind. The skin of his palms felt like it had been scraped over asphalt. On his forehead, the makeup felt dry and cracking across a widening band of irritation. But moving his legs as he walked forward brought such relief that Howard ignored his other pains and kept his hands shoved in his pockets. He would just have to let his skin alone for right now. He practiced forgetting that anything was wrong, pretending he was a piece of the darkness. The faster he walked, the more his body quieted. Howard went down to Filment Street, turning left, and counted the newly lit streetlights as he went along, to center himself.

Storefronts were closed for the evening. He watched his passing reflection overlaid with brassy gilded letters in a dark window—just a tall shadow passing before registering any kind of definition. Neon signs still hissed a red welcome into a few dives. Other apartment buildings seemed mostly quiet, just the sweet tones of someone's record player drifting over the breeze through a second-floor window screen. The buildings seemed taller with the streets vacant and still. Howard imagined being the last man on earth, a wanderer observing the artifacts of an abandoned city. His muscles felt smooth as he walked, the disconcerting buzz now replaced with something like liquid sweetness that grew with each step. It was a fine feeling.

Eleven streetlights went by. Howard noticed a flicker of white movement out of the corner of his eye. A paper flyer fluttered in the breeze, stapled to a post, crumpled by wind, written in a child's hard crayon scrawl. Howard walked over to it: LOST GOD, it said. Below, there was a phone number and a crude illustration of a long-eared black-and-white dog. Howard's mouth twitched. *Lost God,* he repeated in his head. He tried to think of a deity, sitting somewhere, knowing about his fadeaway skin. He imagined this unseen force worrying over the missing dog and trying to brush it home with an omnipotent hand. Could there be, somewhere in the cosmic order, warm arms holding this world that was, in turn, held in the arms of satellites? Did some power still whisper a lullaby to us from afar? Howard didn't know. But he noticed the church as if in answer; it was tucked into the next street corner, all heavy stone and stained glass. The building impelled him, tugged him forward from his cheekbones. One more streetlight down and there he was, in front of the grand steps and a thick double door at the front of the church. Glancing around at the empty streets, Howard thought about how the heavy door might feel to open. Surely it would be locked. But the strange emptiness of the streets and the trembling high of his body's response to movement urged him. Or maybe it was just loneliness. He hardly knew, but he climbed the steps lightly and pulled faithlessly on the iron handle.

The door swung open, yawning into darkness until Howard's eyes adjusted.

He moved deeper into the dark atrium, aware of every small noise that seemed to echo no matter how still he was, the rustle of cloth, his slow breaths. The doors to the sanctuary were propped open, framing the long rows of pews. A candle flame illuminated a red glass lantern hanging by a bronze chain from the ceiling near the altar. The only other light came from three rows of white votives sitting in small glass cups on a low table, flickering deep within the church. It was empty.

Everything smelled of damp oak and incense. Howard stepped past the glass doors and into the cavernous old sanctuary. He hadn't been in a church since he was a boy. Traces of the streetlamp glow filtered through the stained-glass windows, dusting the altar area with light. Howard ran his hand along the polished surface of the wooden pews, brushing his hood back off his head. He sat down in the middle of the second row, breathing in the heavy air, considering the crucifix: a man carved of marble, benevolent and tormented, bleeding and triumphant. Howard found himself wanting to pray, but there weren't any words he knew for prayer. He didn't remember it. The space amplified his breaths, the walls teasing them from his throat. Howard started to whisper the only religious song he knew, until the sound started coming forth. "Ave," he sang. "Maria." Voice shaking, forehead pressed against the back of the pew in front of him, he began to let his voice go, bursting out the tune's long notes, half-inventing the Latin. The acoustics of the tall stone sanctuary magnified his voice until it seemed to fill up the hollow room. Howard kept his eyes closed. He clasped his hands. He sang his pain in a language he didn't know. The whole of his voice warmed through the echoes.

When he fell silent again, Howard's breathing slowed and shook. He opened his eyes to find the carvings of saints around the windows, the ledges, the corners of the walls; his witnesses. A feeling of certainty swept upon him like a cloak. He felt the air around him in a closer way. But the windows seemed to rattle.

Then, a thought came into Howard's consciousness like a strangely colored piece of mail with a forgotten yet familiar return address—a novelty, a quick shock, a turning over in the brain, an anxious tearing open. Hands still clutching one another, Howard looked down at his wrists peeking from the edge of his sleeves. He strained to see in the dim light, but it was unmistakable—the ordinarily precise red tangle of veins and tissue showed dark burgundy spots swirling and bruising like ink blots in water under the skin. He was shaking. He saw the corners of searching stems emerge from behind the statues until the vines fattened, encircling saints in dark leaves. He looked to the ceiling and saw the moon shining, impossibly, through it. The moonlight hit the vines and inflamed them with growth. Howard watched them climb, rustling and dense over the high walls, smother the altar, and burst into bloom. The flowers swelled open, sepal to petal to filaments stretching wide in ache and orison. His vision began to wane. Unconsciousness tugged at him. He fought it.

He stood and staggered back through the sanctuary, small white flowers winding up out of fissures in the floor as he crossed them. With each step, from bud to petal they emerged to lay his path. He bolted out of the church in terror. The large wooden door creaked behind him as he returned to the sidewalk. He looked to the sky.

The moon was gone. The wind picked up, with clouds rolling in fast. Wind whipped Howard's hair straight back from his face. Small gusts accelerated to an all-out gale. Even though he was blocks from the lake, Howard could hear the rise of its guttural roar. It was a black, raging sound. Howard saw no one—not a person, not a single car. Only the rage of the sky, still growing.

Howard took long, urgent strides toward home. He couldn't remember the number of streetlights anymore, but let his body move on its own. Pieces of litter tumbled down the road, and he felt the wind heavy against his chest. He flipped his hood back up, tightening the drawstrings. The wind gave birth to a burst of rain that pummeled the pavement. Fat drops blown by the wind slapped over Howard's face. His melting make-up came away in the water and streamed down his neck.

He began to run.

Howard sprinted through the city streets, through the downpour, like a man possessed. This was a mistake, he thought. He cursed him-self, exhaling hard, thighs pumping, booted feet striking the wet ground. He shut his clear eyelids against the pelting rain, watching droplets hit through a network of pink webbing with each surging step. He was struck by the thought that his eyelids kept getting lighter—would he soon have to bandage his eyes to sleep? He fled swiftly, head down and disoriented, like a wounded deer.

He breathed hard, tugged his hood further down to shield his fore-head, and finally the apartment building loomed up as he ran the final thirty paces.

He started to dive for the door, but saw, too late, that someone was coming outside.

Howard immediately turned to the side and tucked his head down. Under the hood, against the pelting rain, it wouldn't seem that strange, would it? Jo emerged from the lobby door into the downpour, a red um-brella at the ready in one hand and a garbage bag heavy with clinking glass in the other.

25

JO'S WIDE RED UMBRELLA CLICKED open and unfurled. It nearly tugged right out of her hand in the gusting wind. She recognized Howard's tall form approaching right away, even with his hood flipped up and pulled low over his brow, his clothes soaked. It was raining harder outside than she'd thought it was, really pelting. She kept the garbage bag lifted an inch off the wet sidewalk. Between the umbrella and the wind and the long, slicing drops, she thought she saw Howard's face just before he turned away. She recoiled, heart pounding. His face looked red and slick, like the skin had been peeled off. But then she realized that it was just an unsettling trick of her eyes. With the streetlight coming through the veil of her cherry-colored umbrella's waterproof nylon, the puddles on the ground below her glowed red as blood. Only water, she told her still-banging heart.

"Hey, Jo," he mumbled, rushing around her and cranking the door open.

Only Howard.

"Hey!" She yelled over the rain, turning her head back. "Did you get my note?" But he was already inside and out of sight. She knew, at least, that her note was no longer taped to his door. He must have read it. No matter. He probably just wanted to get inside and out of the rain. She could catch him later. She was heartily buzzed on the last of her whiskey anyhow, and moving slowly. Another great night alone.

There was no way around the puddles, so Jo just lightly stepped through them, letting the water wash over her sandaled feet. She carted her clinking bag out to the dumpster on the side of the building. With the rain coming in sheets over the edge of her umbrella, she peered around to the parking lot. Howard's green truck was still there. She imagined herself tooling up Highway 61 in that thing, windows open and deafening FM radio cranked, jostling at each bump that rattled the dash. What was more suited to a free and capable life than a woman with a truck? She could drive out to the state parks. She could have a German shepherd dog riding in the back. She could fill the truck bed with pillows and a quilt and watch fireworks while lying on her back. Hell, she might be able to fit a canoe in there. That truck had an engine that could make things worth her while. It had wheels that could roll over snow, if she was still here in Duluth by then.

The storm was blowing sideways now. The stubborn rain pricked Jo's nose and wrist and speckled her jeans. The wind was a little frightening, continuing to catch the umbrella in an attempt to whisk it from her grip.

The wet-looking face of flesh and bone pushed its way forward again in her mind. She knew that she couldn't have seen what she thought she saw, but it still disturbed her.

It was just Howard, the man she met the day before. Not a peeled-back face and startling, long skeleton teeth. That was impossible. Her mind wasn't clear. She told herself that she needed to sleep. She hurried back inside, but couldn't shake the idea of the skinless man.

I must be out-of-my-mind drunk, she thought. Out of it again.

By the time she was back in the house, time began to drift, and her gut filled with shame. She couldn't even remember sitting back down on the couch. She was still wet. She rubbed her eyes with her cold palms. Wasn't she just taking out the recycling? How much had she had? The red umbrella lay dripping on the rug by the doorway, taunting her.

She told herself that she wouldn't feel this way by morning. That face, some manifestation of her own decaying grief—it would fade back down into her sheets and melt in the sunlight. An alarm would sound. Maybe she would share a laugh with her neighbor in the hallway as she left for work. She realized how chilled she felt in the rain-damp clothes. Her eyes strayed to the side, and she noticed her phone on the coffee table, blinking. Her parents' home phone number again. She asked herself why the hell not and pressed "Return call." It only took two rings for a warm male voice to pick up.

"Dad?" Her lower lip tensed.

He was frantic and happy and everything a father should be when he talks to his daughter, asking if she was doing all right, what her place looked like, if her job was going well, when they could visit. A fumbling clicking sound and her mother was in on the call, too, having picked up the cordless phone in the bedroom, the care in her voice as thick and real as a warm cake sitting on the kitchen counter. Jo recounted the details of her environments, mapping her reality for listening ears, so suddenly feeling the home and routine and comfort she'd been avoiding since arriving in the city. Ike hopped up on her lap and meowed loudly enough that they could hear him all the way in Colesburg and laugh. His work then complete, the cat dove into the back of the closet, rustling noisily into a cardboard box.

"Look, I'm so sorry I haven't called you," Jo said then. Instantaneous protests of love from both parents reassured her. She felt cherished, hushed, protected, and completely unworthy of it. She was so precious to them, and it killed her. But she just kept talking, and uncorked a flow of words that she worried might sound incoherent as she tried to filter it through an optimistic tone. "I feel like I'm really settling in here. Things really make a lot of sense to me here"—lies erected to dam the wave of guilt for her drunken, irresponsible default mode, for omitting the news that she had damaged a woman's vehicle and disturbed a neighbor's peace, for not admitting that she felt more unstable in every way than she ever had, for leaving in the first place, for feeling like she could fix herself alone. But the word "love" slipped out in her goodbye, and that was honest. She loved her faraway parents so much that it crushed her. Maybe her desire to stand on her own, to define herself, was faulted. Maybe there was nothing to define. She longed for home, just as she had in the dorms as an undergrad. And, just as she had then, she told herself to grow up. Had anything happened to mark these past ten years of her life? She didn't want to acknowledge the obvious fact of it: she was exactly the damn same as she had always been.

Jo placed the phone back on the coffee table, huddling in the wide divot she'd nested into the floral cushions of the old couch. Cozy yellow lamplight surrounded her. She wrapped her tattered quilt around her shoulders. The shadowy overlaid image of Howard's bloody face still stood at the edge of her thoughts.

Maybe she needed another drink—the liquor might steady her, she reasoned, get her back in touch with what was real. She wanted more dark whiskey in her plastic tumbler. I need just a little more tonight, she told herself, heading to the kitchen. She told herself that it was not the time for a sobriety commitment, not now, when things were so hard. But she had forgotten already—the whiskey was gone. All her alcohol was gone. She swore, and turned the faucet to blast, holding her tumbler under the cold water from the tap. Half of it landed in the cup. Good enough.

Returning to the couch and setting the cup coasterless on the oak table with the wobbly leg, she snatched her laptop and flung it open with a grand sweep of her hand, fantasizing absurdly about being a noir detective getting ready to crack a case. She searched, wading through the results of online queries that accumulated into frightening poetry: *skin diseases / skin color loss / alcohol hallucinations / see muscle through skin / can drinking make you hallucinate / rare illnesses skin / man without skin dream meaning.*

Withdrawal from alcohol addiction, she knew, could cause a form of psychosis in rare cases. Did her feeble attempts to quit in the past few weeks trigger some kind of episode? The seesawing binges and droughts she'd been following couldn't be good for anyone's body, she supposed. But had she hallucinated? She decided that was unlikely, took another sip of water and toasted the air with a desperate frivolity.

She continued searching late into the night, muddling through abstracts of medical articles until she didn't even remember what she was really looking for. Fatigue crashed over her. The most she could do was double-check her alarm on her phone before slumping into sleep right there on the couch, the lights still on, and Ike, emerged from his closet den, purring atop her feet.

26

THE NEXT MORNING, CUSTOMERS FLUTTERED in and out of Trenton Floral at a steady pace. Jo, Tonya, Ruth, and a new girl named Callie bustled to grab arrangements from the cooler, jot down requests for last-minute prom orders over the phone, and snatch up gardenia, hibiscus, and aloe plants for customers. One wrinkled man in overalls winked at Jo as she wrapped up a bunch of irises for him and thanked her for doing such a nice job. His wife would love them, he said. Jo nodded and smiled through the pulsing throb at her temples. She was confused about the night before. She remembered being fixated on the face of blood and vein and cord she thought she'd seen. That seemed ridiculous now, especially in comparison to her more immediate problem of a massive headache.

As hectic as the floral shop around her was, Jo moved slowly through a sludge of pain. She knew she needed to stop wasting her nights swimming in booze. It was a problem, one that she had to fix. She told herself she could do better. She could start by doing her best at work today, even with the loud ache that pulsed behind her eyes. She told herself it was pain that she deserved.

As she continued fetching things and interacting with customers, she arrived on a thought that rooted through all the others. She hated being lonely. At least, she thought, she was no longer alone while being alongside somebody else. Small comfort. She had to start looking out for herself. She no longer had anyone else to blame. She stuffed colorful tissue paper into a box around a vased arrangement for a customer, brought cellophane up around it, and tied the top with a ribbon. The bright flowers beneath the wrapping looked cheerful. The woman who bought it sighed as Jo placed it in her waiting hands.

The rush of walk-in customers started to abate, and Jo moved to the processing counter tucked in the back corner of the shop. She grabbed a pair of cutters from behind the back counter and split the plastic tie that fastened the cover of a fresh box of carnations. She heaved the bunches of brilliant gold and tangerine, wrapped tightly and still smelling of dusty, sweet Columbian humidity. Tonya joined Jo at the counter, setting down a large container for a dish garden. She placed river stones just so and tucked small succulents into place in the soil, creating a tiny forest beneath her hands. Jo filled vases with fresh water at the faucet.

"Hey, Tonya," Jo asked, "Have you ever heard of . . . like a sickness where the person loses all the color in their skin? Like you can see their muscles and stuff through their skin?"

Tonya's laugh was like a round bell. "What are you talking about?" Her nose scrunched up.

"I don't know. I mean, I saw something strange yesterday. Or maybe I just thought I did. I can't get it out of my head. Isn't that weird?" She positioned the stem ends of the carnations over the trash can and started lopping them off with her cutters, the fresh sap dewily oozing through the pithy stems.

Tonya stopped what she was doing and turned to Jo. Her eyebrows drew closer together. "Are you OK?" She was smiling, but she wasn't joking. The window was open for Jo to admit something if she wanted to. She cleared her throat instead.

Tonya lifted a tiny peace lily out of its plastic pot and started breaking up the root ball, her fingers moving delicately through fibers like she was untangling a child's hair. "I mean, really," she said, as she made an opening in the soil of the dish garden and settled the lily inside. "Do we need to be worried about you?"

"No, no," Jo protested. "Forget I said anything about it. I mean I'm not saying I don't have problems, but, yeah, I think maybe I haven't been sleeping enough or something."

"Hey." Tonya stopped her work to square her shoulders toward Jo. Her eye contact made Jo want to cry. "We take care of our own here," she said. "We all got our own problems, right?"

"Yes. But someone . . . I don't know." Jo waved her hand as if she could fling the feeling away. "I'm trying to handle what I've got going on." She wanted to smack herself for the tears she could hear mounting in her voice.

"Well, listen, we can help you if you ever want to talk."

Jo nodded and Tonya left it at that. They continued working quietly, in a collegial pas de deaux. Tonya lifted, placed, spun, gathered, pressed. Jo pulled stems up high and thrust bunches of them into the water, foggy with dissolving flower food, of the thick crystal cooler vases that lined the counter. Leaves and petals were velvet under her fingers. The hum of conversation from customers and other employees drifted up along the high windows of the shop. Once, when Jo turned to lift a new box up to the counter, she found Tonya's golden-brown eyes looking at her as if there was a lot more to say.

"I hope you don't feel like it's your fault for whatever you're struggling with," Tonya said. "A lot of people have a hard time, you know? Like my mom—my mom had problems with her health. It gave her trouble her whole life, wrecked her lungs and gave her a lot of pain before she passed. And it wasn't anything she did; she was just sick. It killed me to see her like that."

Jo paused in her work, feeling the trust that Tonya was offering, a hand extended. "Wow, I'm so sorry to hear that about your mom," Jo said. "That sounds really hard. Nobody should have to go through that."

"No, they should not." Tonya was lost in memory now, in reverence. "But she—she was a great woman, you know? Powerful. It didn't get her all the way; she raised her family just the same until the end. When I was pregnant with Christopher, I was scared I might not be able to be as strong as she was if I got sick like she did. I worried constantly. But I leaned on my husband and my friends when it was too much. I made it through motherhood. So far, at least. Ah, that crazy boy." She laughed, adding a spray of leaf shine to the plants in front of her. She put her hand on Jo's shoulder. "So, did you get your incident from the other day straightened out with Sarah? Like I said, I'm sure that the shop's insurance can help cover the damage. It's not a big deal." She picked up the finished dish garden to place it in the front window display.

"No, no. It's my responsibility. I just really feel like I should take ownership of it. Anyway, we made an agreement that I could pay her back in installments," said Jo, thinking back to the evening at the pub with Sarah. "She said that she stays near a waterfall area that hikers visit sometimes. I'm probably going to go up there."

"Not Gooseberry Falls?" asked Tonya.

"No. No, it's not a big one like that. I had to get a special map from the guy at the outfitter to even figure out where it was, but he seemed to be familiar with it. Moss Falls, I think?" Jo smoothed her black hair down where the cowlick always stuck up in back. Her headache was finally starting to clear.

"Wow, never heard of it. I've been to Beaver Falls, High Falls . . . I'm trying to think." The door chimed as a stout, red-faced woman entered the shop. Tonya smiled at her. "Hello!"

Jo remembered the husky, amber sound of Sarah's voice that night at the pub. "She said it wasn't really very big—might not even be in a real park. I think it's just near her property." She lifted the vase overflowing with finished carnations to bring them to the cooler. "She said it was up the shore. So, I guess that means Highway 61." Tonya didn't respond;

she was already tending to the customer, who was looking for a bouquet. Jo thought about the money for the car repair, and her cheeks flushed. She hoped it wouldn't be very expensive. She planned to give Sarah fifty dollars to start and then wait to hear more. She was also trying to buy Howard's truck, not to mention rent and groceries. She had a cash reserve from her savings, but it was bleeding quickly. She'd spent too much furnishing her apartment with garage sale finds. And there was the booze. Still, she had money coming in from her Trenton paychecks—not a lot, but enough. Jo wanted to do right by Sarah. She wanted to follow through for once. No excuses. She'd look at her money tonight, take out what she could at an ATM, and find a way to get the cash to Sarah. She could do that. It was something that she could take off her conscience.

Ruth swooped up beside Jo, fresh off the phone. She glared at the receiver for a moment. "These people are out of their minds sometimes," she whispered to Jo, shaking her head. She was holding an order sheet with dozens of crossed-off and rewritten notes about colors and pricing. Jo smiled as the older woman lightly tapped her on the shoulder with the scribbled order sheet. "What's new with you, Jo?" She asked.

Jo smiled at Ruth. "Not much, I've mostly just been hanging out with my cat." Her reply made Ruth cackle with good humor.

27

HEARING A KNOCK ON HIS door early in the morning, Howard felt confident about who he'd find on the other side. Jo was there, waiting in the hallway, leaning against the wall, glancing and swiping at her phone. Howard's immaculately concealed face peeked out, and she brightened. "Hey, again!" There he was, his lips perhaps a bit too rosy, the glinting tan packed tight with foundation. But the fear Howard had scratched across his memory of seeing Jo in the rain the other night muted into relief. She showed no sign of worry. She was simply looking at him like he was an ordinary man, and he relaxed in her gaze.

"Hi." Jo was raising her eyebrows at him, her expression on its way to scolding. Then again, he thought, she had reason to be. She really wanted that damn truck, it seemed, and he hadn't answered the notes she kept sticking on his door. Or the two follow-up emails she'd sent. Now she was here to reckon, in black jeans and a dandelion-yellow blouse with a geometric print. "I think you know why I'm here," she said. She shook her head, and a smile broke across her face.

Her eyes looked the same as they had on the first night they met. He knew, because he had the Polaroid of her, still sitting on his kitchen table. He'd grown to know her face. Now, seeing her again, he felt a rush of something sweet, but also a shifting unease.

He'd been closed up in his apartment since the evening walk two days ago. He'd been scared, telling himself he couldn't go out again. It was too exposed. Someone could see him. Someone could take a video. Someone could set off a hunt, a viral social media spotlight that could thrust him into spectacle and terror. He had to stay hidden. But his efforts to focus kept failing. Writing endlessly in the dark hole of his apartment no longer sated him. The maddening itch to get outside again had already resurged; he could not quell it or quiet it, this compulsion that constantly pressed at his body. It frightened him. Now, with his apartment door cracked open to the world outside, it was all he could do to just stand still. He looked at Jo.

"So, is the truck still for sale or not?" Her smile was smug, but still open, and she shifted her weight to her other leg, tilting her hip up. "I can pay you some right away—cash. And the rest when I can, over the next couple months. I'll be honest with you, it might take a while, but if you don't have another buyer . . . I'll need a test drive, though. If it's still for sale, that is." She tucked a hand in her back pocket.

Part of him wondered if he'd ever get a penny out of her.

A month ago, Howard would have been happy to send her and his truck on their way together, but the thought of letting it go now jostled him in a way he couldn't really place. Maybe it was some sort of survival instinct, to hold on to every asset. He thought for the briefest moment of driving North, ever North, like the creature from Mary Shelley's novel upon his dogsled. The truck could save him that way. And it made for a better image, a better way to the pyre, than some self-conscious sedan kept precious and scratchless in the garage. One cannot make a pyre of one's life in a sedan, he thought.

Jo was talking again, but his thoughts were too scattered to keep up with what she was saying. God, she was thin, he thought. She was thin in a non-physical way that made him think of his own fading away, except it was like an energy around her. It was a frayed confidence, a hissing leak in the buoyancy that made him suddenly see her as someone who was friendly, but who was one wrong idea away from setting something on fire. In that, he saw himself and so, though that other part of him wanted to drive North until the gas and his own will ran out, the more present part of him dared himself to give her that truck.

"A test drive, sure," he mumbled, finally. "It's the least I could do. I'm sorry I've been so hard to reach." How would he do it? He wasn't sure. It didn't matter. Looking at her made him reckless. His muscles hummed. He didn't care.

"That would be wonderful." She seemed pleased. "I have something I need to drop off up the shore for a friend. Could we do that? Maybe make a day of it, do some hiking? I mean, only if you want to. I can bring my own camera this time." That smile again. She looked like she could devour him. Had she seen his real face that night in the rain? It made him feel like crying. His body was screaming out for movement now—he clutched the side of the door harder, willing himself still.

"Sure," he said.

They arranged to meet out by the truck the next day, in the late afternoon after Jo was done with work. It was simple. It was as if he was living a normal life. She smiled and waved, went inside, back to her own little world across the hall from his.

He didn't necessarily need to sell her the truck, if he changed his mind, he thought. He could only hope that Jo would keep her dark eyes on the road.

28

THE NEXT DAY, A GROUP of gulls flew in a row across the sky, heading east. Howard watched them as he stood waiting for Jo in the bright parking lot, wearing all black. Dark pants, boots, and a black turtleneck. It was warm in the afternoon sun, but not sweltering. The breeze was cool. He'd spent all morning getting ready after a long and punishing night of writing. Even though his skin felt raw when he touched it too much, he had applied, partially scrubbed off, and reapplied his pigmented mask several times, buffing and dabbing and setting his face until his tormented skin was smooth, matte, and uniformly opaque. Hours of practice over the past weeks had made him precise, able to contour the curves of the face and neck like a sculptor. If someone was at least a few feet away and didn't know any better, he might look like any other man. He wore biking gloves to cover his hands. Just his foundation-caked fingertips poked out. They weren't as perfect as the work on his face, but he supposed he could keep them hidden if he needed to. He had pockets. Still, nerves laced his breath. Here he was, outside in the daylight. To his shock, nobody had paid him any mind so far—neighbors walking to their cars hadn't even glanced in his direction. Maybe this would be all right, he thought. He tried to look unobtrusive and casual as he walked the length of the parking lot, back and forth, trying desperately not to touch his face, grateful for the wash of relief in his joints as he moved.

Jo walked up right on time. She was wearing a green hiking shirt and she carried a corduroy backpack. She had denim shorts on. She looked happy. "You ready to show me this beast?" she said, gesturing to the truck.

"Here it is," he said. He hoped she couldn't hear his voice shaking. "She's a 2001 F250. Little over two hundred thousand miles on her. Feel free to do a walk around, check everything out." He stepped aside to let her.

Jo ran her fingers over the faded seafoam green pinstripe running through the center of the paint job, looked at the slight reddish flaking around the curve of the underbody in a sunburn of rust. She saw the dents in the bed and touched the wisps of cotton stuffing that poked out of two tiny rips in the upholstery of the driver's seat. She felt her heart shrug into the truck. She couldn't wait to get her hands on the steering wheel.

She swung her backpack—which carried a water bottle, her camera, bottles of bug spray, the maps, and the money for Sarah—into the rear storage seat. She looked back to a questioning glance from Howard. Her neighbor was decidedly weird. Now that she saw him in true daylight for the first time, it seemed like he was wearing makeup. Maybe it wasn't his face that looked so different, but rather what he put on the surface. Maybe he just liked wearing makeup; there were guys like that. Or maybe he was a drag performer. Maybe the face he had hidden from her the other night was a part of his act. Maybe that was why he was so skittish—maybe he was unsure how she would react. Whatever it was, it didn't bother Jo at all. It made her like him more. Who knew what he had been through in his life? Who knew that about anybody? Besides, that turtleneck did look good on him. He had a waiting grace about him, like a dancer, she thought. And anyway, spending time with Howard was the way she was going to get this gorgeous, gorgeous truck. So, she coaxed the man with the radiantly strange face to hop into the passenger side of the Ford as she climbed behind the wheel and slid the seat forward.

Howard fastened his seat belt, reached the keys over and dropped them in her palm. "Let's see how you like it," he said. She grinned, shut the door neatly, and twisted the key, listening as the engine chugged heartily to life. She put her phone in the cup holder with the GPS set to the closest trailhead she could estimate when she checked it against the label for Moss Falls on her map from the outfitter. She felt certain that she could find the house with the brown Oldsmobile parked in front, but even if she couldn't, maybe they'd at least get to see the waterfall.

She tooled through town with her thoughts rotating happily. It was nice to be up high in the driver's seat, floating above the road. Before long, she was easing north onto Highway 61. Howard didn't say much, other than to offer a few small functional instructions about the dashboard. "Do you mind if we listen to the radio?" she asked. "I'd like to hear how the sound system works." He laughed.

"It's pretty crappy," he said, and turned the knob. She begged to differ. The old speakers had sound filtering through a sweet overcrackle, blissfully bumping along to a rhythmic piano riff until a soaring voice struck pure above it. The lyrics spoke of stars in an endless sky, the willingness to be torn apart for a glimpse of a lover in the constellations.

Howard had never liked the song, but he kept that to himself. Less out of politeness and more because the song was making sense right at that moment, just there. He saw a woman who was seeing herself in the lines of the road, in the gulls sweeping over the lake, in the faint reflection of her short shock of dark hair in the windshield. It was all Jo. He was warm and full of sun from the window. The action of the truck speeding along lulled him. He forgot himself and closed his eyes, letting her drive. He hadn't known it, but this truck had always been hers.

His head lay back against the seat. Light bisected and flashed through the window as the truck passed under the alternating shadows of trees and the light of open sky. His eyelashes made fragile half circles; his lips were wet, reddish, and parted. When the truck jostled over a bump, his hair fell across his forehead.

THEY DROVE FOR longer than Howard had expected, but it occurred to him that Jo hadn't specified how far she wanted to go, just that she wanted to run an errand for a friend who lived near a hiking trail. He'd been quiet for most of the drive, and she kept flicking her eyes sideways at him. He willed himself to pay attention, to shake himself out of the sleepiness that the warm sun was keeping over him. He pushed up straighter in his seat and fought the urge to rub at his eyes.

"So, you just moved in not that long ago, right?" he asked. She nodded. They passed under a short tunnel cut right into the towering Silver Creek Cliff. They rumbled through to the other side and back to the sunshine. The lake, to the right, was a perfect blue expanse.

"Yeah," Jo said. "I needed a fresh start. I'm from Iowa. Needed a change of scenery. I left my husband—" Her voice broke on the last word.

"Oh." Howard kept his eyes on the road. He decided that there was no good response, so he left it at that. The truck bumped over a small pothole. Jo winced.

"My marriage is over," she said. "Plain and simple. There was nothing holding us together. It's hard for me to say this out loud, but—I've come to understand. My husband didn't want to be with me. I don't know if he ever did. I tried to be better, to love him harder, to do all these things to make him remember. But I couldn't do it. So I'm here, I guess, wondering how any of it happened, how I ended up carrying the wedding gown he took off me through a parking lot and shoving it in a Goodwill donation bin, how I could've fucked up that badly. And now I'm just trying to keep myself above water. I'm sorry. Is it all right that I'm talking with you about all this?"

"It's all right," Howard said. He felt the weight of her warmth beside him in a new way.

She gestured to the lake and cleared her throat. "Anyway, forget all that. Did you know there are something like three hundred shipwrecks in Lake Superior? I saw that on a poster in Duluth. It's not just the one from that song."

"The *Edmund Fitzgerald!*" He bent forward in his seat and tapped his hand against his knee. "It's so strange that you bring that up. I just wrote a piece about Lake Superior shipwrecks for a tourism website. People around here are really into that history. The research was so absorbing, just thinking about those huge ships, marvels of engineering with experienced captains. A lot of them just disappeared. The weather turns suddenly, rogue waves start hitting, and they're lost with all hands. Gone to the bottom. Some of them still haven't been found."

Jo squinted at the road. After a moment, she asked, "How could anyone hope to mourn something like that?"

Howard shook his head. "Some people used to say that the ghosts of shipwrecked sailors still walk the woods in places where their boats struck the rocks."

"Ghosts?"

"Yes. Just a story."

"You're a writer?"

"Yeah, that's how I pay the bills."

Jo made a small sound of recognition, then dropped the conversation. She pulled her lips in between her teeth and bobbed her head back and forth to crack her neck. She rubbed her right hand on her thigh.

Little tufts of Howard's hair flickered against his neck. The air buffeted his partially rolled-down passenger-side window. He thought about the sailors on the night of the fray, frantically shouting their last prayers, waves of elemental cold crashing over their ship's bow. It was hard to believe that the smooth sunlit surface he was gazing at was the same lake that could hold such horrors. He summoned the bravest thing he could.

"Jo."

"What?"

"To lose you—he must have been blind."

Silence floated down between them, both staring at the road, blazing northward along the coast. Yellow wildflowers blurred up from the rails along the cliffside, a delicate foreground to the reddish gray stone that tapered down beyond the road. He wasn't sure she had heard him, but he couldn't ask. The moment was too fragile to hold onto, so he let it float gently out the window and over the shimmering lake in the distance. Another offering to the depths.

"How much further to your coworker's place?" he asked some time later. "What was it you needed to bring her?"

"Should be soon," said Jo. "I owe her some money, and I thought we could drop it off. The directions I have aren't very good, but I know she lives near a waterfall." She tilted her phone toward her to glance at the GPS. "We're getting close, and I'll definitely recognize her car if it's out. I guess this is kind of long for a test drive."

"No," he said. "I'm enjoying it." They weren't the right words, but they were close enough. The sun glinted in her hair.

Jo gestured to the tiny backseat of the cab with her thumb. "Could you grab my backpack and get the map out of there?" He complied, touching as little as possible with his makeup-caked hands, zipper lightly grasped and pulled by the very ends of his fingertips. He found the map and gently laid it on his lap. He noticed pencil marks and notations written by hand on the paper.

"I thought you were using your GPS," he said.

"Well, I sort of am. I couldn't find anyone who's heard of Moss Falls except for a guy at the camping store where I got all that bug repellent that's in my backpack. When I asked him, he took out a photocopied map and started marking these different hiking routes. He starred a bunch of waterfalls, too, and I guess Moss Falls is kind of a lesser-known one. He circled it for me." Howard unfolded the paper all the way, trying to make sense of the pencil scrawls and the occasional arrow. This was more involved than he had expected, and it made him nervous.

A spike of heat cracked through Howard's bones, demanding movement; the forward lurch of the truck suddenly felt insufficient and maddening. His body needed to move, to walk freely, to escape the small, suffocating space of the cab. He reminded himself that they would soon be on the trail. He could make it. Just a little longer. He shifted in his seat. The seatbelt pulled tight across his chest.

Jo checked her phone. "Damn. Looks like my battery is running a little low." She turned to Howard. "You have yours?"

Howard felt his pocket and cursed at himself inwardly. "No, I must have left my phone back at the apartment."

"Oh. Well, don't worry, we've got enough battery to get us there. I wish I could just call Sarah, but I guess she doesn't give her number out. Anyway, I'm sure it won't be too hard to find her house. She has this ancient brown station wagon with wood paneling. Believe me, it's hard to miss."

Howard nodded. The truck hummed along. He pictured himself leaping out of the passenger door and flying into the woods to run along the dark paths winding beneath the towering red pines. All over, his skin bristled with rising pain. As he let it overtake him, he thought of another day, some day when he could no longer endure, when he would not be able to go back to the apartment. When he could no longer stop walking without going mad. Maybe he could come back to the same spot, up here. He could just leave everything in his apartment paused without him, the ships in their bottles ever sailing on, all deadlines met, phone turned off and left at the desk. He could just keep walking and walking, until he walked right out of anyone's memory. It might be a cold day, windy. Like a being between man and creature, he could pick his way along the landscape, always moving, alone and meditative. He could live there, unnoticed, learning to survive. No one would seek him. And at the end of his days, he'd just be quietly collapsed, lightly arranged, for the deer to pass with gentle avoidance. The rustling of leaves marking his last moments, nobody knowing, just one star sputtering out. Would he think of her then? The idea was comforting, that one warm day could be summoned back at the end of one small life.

He started feeling faint, and his head lolled heavily to the right without his control.

"Howard!" Jo's hand flew off the steering wheel to touch his shoulder and then swiftly back, correcting the truck back into the lane. Lines like a windshield fracture shot across Howard's vision, then faded. Just as soon, he was alert again, heart jumping.

"I'm all right," he said, shaken. He wildly attempted to mask his distress. "Just had a sharp pain in my head—it's gone. Sorry, Jo."

"Should I pull over?" she asked. The color had drained from her lips.

"No, God, I'm sorry—just too much sun, maybe. I've had some, uh, minor medical issues lately. My body has been overly sensitive. A little carsick. It's passed. I'm fine now." The motion of the truck seemed to slow compared to the reeling in his vision. But it dissolved, and he steadied.

"You're positive?"

"Promise. Sorry to scare you."

"OK. Just let me know if you change your mind."

Jo nervously watched the center of the road. Out the window, the pines were taller, the woods thicker. Endless shadow forms that could have been creatures flickered by between the tree trunks. "I think we're getting close," Jo said. Her foot weighed a little lighter on the accelerator. She took the exit. They started seeing more wooden, hand-painted signs on the side of the road, and Jo nearly bounced in her seat with recognition when she pointed to one that read MOSS FALLS on a small piece of repurposed pallet wood with a green painted arrow to the right.

Down the winding gravel road, there was a half-cleared grassy space that seemed to be intended for parking, though whether this was public or private property, Jo couldn't tell. Nobody else was around, just a crow lazily calling into the late afternoon sunlight. She pulled in and shut off the truck.

Howard rushed to unclick his seat belt and get out of the door. He felt his lungs open wider, his breathing come easier, the moment he stood. Jo got out, too, and stretched, her arms folding over her head as she tilted her jaw to the sky. "Wow," she said, looking up at the stands of red pine and black spruce, and ghostly white birches further on. "Beautiful, isn't it?" He nodded. She looked him up and down, still worried. "Hey, seriously, if you're not feeling well, I can just run up the path a bit and see if we're in the right place." She handed the keys back over to him.

"I'm coming with you," said Howard, tucking the keys into his pocket. He sucked in a deep breath. "The fresh air feels good. And we came all this way." She narrowed her eyes but found a smile. She stepped closer to him, touched his arm gently. He could feel the warmth of her hand. The hushed energy of Jo's body was, it occurred to him somehow, much like rain.

"Let's see what kind of trouble we can get into," she said. She took the backpack from the truck and set it on the ground, then lifted her camera out, detached the lens cap and tucked it into her back pocket. She bowed her head to sling the camera strap around her neck. She double-checked her settings for shutter speed and ISO. After spraying her legs and arms generously with bug repellent, sending a lemony chemical smell into the lazy breeze, she strapped the pack on with both straps. She and Howard could hear the tumble of the river already, coming from the same direction as a narrow path where the grass looked tamped down by footfalls. Long stems brushed past their calves as they followed the path, and the stirring forest air was foggy with warmth.

29

SARAH SAT ON THE METAL folding chair in front of her kitchen table, repacking the same box that she had packed and unpacked seven times since boarding up her windows. She laid the first plate into the box, set down three infinitely creased pieces of tissue paper, and reached for another plate. A thin, apologetic kind of light eked through small gaps in the window boards. She opened the door and latched the screen to let in some air.

She knew exactly how much cash she had tucked away under the loose floorboard in the bedroom and how she would move again. A new ID was already ordered. She would do the exchange outside Ahlborn's within a week, cash in an envelope for a new little plastic falsehood. Same first name, different last.

She had to face it—too many people were becoming familiar here. They knew her face. So often too polite to ask questions even when tempted, these people were starting to creep into her life. She couldn't stop berating herself for speaking so casually to the young woman from the flower shop. Who was she? Who might she talk to? Probably no one and nobody, but there was no sure way to know, and that meant she wasn't safe. Sarah stacked three more plates in the box, each wrapped in tissue. She rose, moved to the cupboard. Mugs were next.

Still, the idea of relocating again tasted metallic. Did she still have the energy for finding a new anonymous hideaway, to cut her hair? Maybe nobody even cared to find her anymore. But she couldn't be sure. What would happen if she stayed? Would she be committed to a behavioral health facility? Fined? Jailed? She'd broken her share of laws in an effort to stay hidden—the thought made her feel sick. Or was it possible that nothing would happen? She was functional. She'd been capably dodging attention for years. She was smart enough. Perhaps she really could live out her days unbothered, here in a cabin that suited her, waiting for the coming and going of leaves and birds as the seasons drifted by. She wished there was a way to accurately quantify the risk.

Peace would not come, though she waited, trying to feel it. The cardboard flaps on the top of the box between her knees splayed open in yearning. But she sat still, unable to yield all the way. The mugs stayed in the cabinet.

Sarah knew if she couldn't put a mug in a box, she could not lift a case of pipettes or the old laryngoscope on the high shelf without falling apart. She couldn't even think about the thin box shoved cockeyed against the furthest corner beneath her bed—old letters, diplomas redacted in permanent marker, the charred paper shreds of the birth certificate she'd mostly burned.

Running, too, was its own kind of risk. Wary and worn, she put her head in her hands. Then she heard the voices.

Two voices. One male and one female. Quiet, but carrying outside on the faint wind.

She walked out behind the house to look and saw flashes of green and black clothing deep in the trees. Only hikers, she told herself, but kept constant watch on them, her wariness accelerating as they moved in and out of her sight.

The water was high, and the sun began to dip into a pink-gold haze behind the trees when the fish and all his brothers saw their mates arrive. Their luminous skin, blurred through the tiers of disrupted water, prompted the slow crescendo of a growing frenzy. The first few brothers rose, swimming in tandem with their partners, clustering together, bellies brushing over backs. The fish turned about in small spaces, drawn in ecstatic coils around each other. The large females were pregnant with the burden they'd carried from so far away, and waved their broad, barbeled heads in expectation.

A flourish of gleaming red gills opened wide, drinking in relief as they loosed their promise against a flurry of eggs. The boundaries of bodies became confused, tails beating and spines breaking the surface of the water as they turned and turned again. The water crashed with them. Soon, the entire bed of the cove awoke with their bursting joy.

The beginning was here. The beginning would always be here.

Part Three

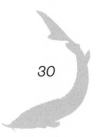

30

THE WOODS COULD FEEL THEM come inside. Jo's strides and Howard's fell into sync. She clutched her camera close to her chest as they moved over the trail, sometimes ducking a branch or stretching a leg over a large root. The click-whirr of her camera shots punctuated their steps as she found pleasing shapes and colors to frame—a dry, white leaf perfectly curled on a bed of spongy soil, a gangly crow peering down from an upper branch before swooping up and away. She wasn't thinking about whiskey. She wasn't thinking about anything other than just moving over the trail and all the brightness of color in the new leaves. The odd, quiet man who walked behind her fit into Jo's landscape unobtrusively. Howard. The man who lived next door. He was different, she admitted to herself. His presence was a slow current wordlessly inviting her to flow into and back out of it, without demand, however she might wish. Standing as he was, the way the light fell, he looked perfect. Through her lens, the air nearest to him seemed charged. Almost like he was disrupting it, or joining it. When she was sure he wasn't watching, she took the shot.

She found a delicate cluster of fiddleheads springing up, stems covered in tiny brown hairs, fronds curled like babies' fists in the newest of greens. She framed the bark of a birch tree in her viewfinder. The birch paper curled away from the trunk in a wealth of layers from charcoal to dove to rose. The abundance of it mesmerized her. She stretched out a hand to touch the ringlets of bark. They felt like nearly nothing, a cascade of surreal softness. Jo began to understand what Cait had told her about the bewitching nature of the North Woods. The air held the first arrival of humidity. She breathed in the forest's exhale.

As the tree cover got thick enough to filter the sunlight, the trammeled grasses of the path gave way to the soil and pine needles of forest floor. Everything smelled of fragrant conifers and leafy wetness. Jo leapt over low parts of the path muddied by the recent rain, caking her boots at the toe and spattering her shins with droplets of mud. Howard followed in long, more careful steps. His presence comforted her. He was kind. She liked that.

When she saw a flash of chestnut in the trees, Jo stopped. As Howard caught up, she turned carefully to whisper to him. "Look, something wild!" He followed the angle of her pointing arm and saw the doe, partially obscured by brush, lowering her fuzzy lips to the grass. The fur on her forehead was dark. Flank and ears quivered. She was a creature of beauty and fear, perfect beneath the gracious downsweep of a branch. It dappled her with shade, her own archway beneath the hazy sun that hung above. A twig cracked, and the doe ran.

Jo turned to Howard. His eyes held her. But then he gestured forward with his arm. "Keep going!" he said, "I have to finish this hike and get back home to sell some lady a truck." He tilted his chin down, averting his eyes, but he was smiling. Jo nodded and started walking more briskly down the trail. She shook her head and grinned to herself.

AS JO CONTINUED to watch the woods through her lens, Howard was content to drink in the sounds of the forest and silently give thanks that her back was to him again.

He felt something strange—the air in his lungs talking to the air that spun about the trees and tender stems, the pulsing of his blood matching the tenor of the sap moving through the trunks. There was a power returning to his muscles. It was like a song in his veins, with drums of flowers coming to bud and a voice layering fractals of pine branches over and over until they deepened to black.

He felt an ease, a wholeness, shift into his body, and he wondered if he had ever felt happier.

31

THEY CAME UPON THE SMALL waterfall as the river turned. A six-foot drop stretched the water over a shelf of rock—jagged, glossy, and black. Moss Falls bubbled down into the curve of the downstream stretch below. Jo raised her camera, eye straining through the viewfinder to frame the right instant. She snapped three quick shutter releases and twisted the lens to zoom. Through the frame, she noticed the dustings of rich green moss and swollen folds of morels growing under the trees along the bank.

Standing far aside to give Jo room to shoot, Howard looked down and noticed a brilliant red streak where makeup had rubbed clean from his index finger. He tightened his fist, folding his fingers into the black material of his biking gloves, and kept walking.

Continuing to follow the river, Jo and Howard walked east toward a place where the trees thinned. The path opened into a clearing where the river folded in upon itself, pooling in a slow-moving inlet. The lake was there too, in the distance just beyond a series of rock formations that stood in a glacial march, spanning their own sense of time. Water gathered in a large crater shape. A shore of smooth stones eased its way to the edge of the slow-lapping estuary.

Turning around to look up at the hill just behind them, Jo caught a glimpse of a small cabin framed by aspen trees. She gestured to Howard, smiling wide. "I bet that's Sarah's place. I think I'll run up there and see."

"Hang on," said Howard. He looked out at the water, transfixed. The view was pristine. The water's surface lay still. The reflected trees, upside down, seemed to sink toward the earth, while the wisps of clouds in that watery mirror looked like the aurora borealis of some other land that was maybe quite near to this one. The golden light of the sun seemed to set the young leaves of certain trees in the image of itself, like living suns. It was the sheer poetry of the earth.

"Yes," Jo said, "You're right."

"What?"

Jo shrugged out of the corduroy backpack, pulled her camera strap off over her head, and nestled the camera in its case inside the bag. The surface beckoned her. She sat down, right on the ground where she was, and started tugging off boots and socks. "Come on," she said to Howard. She held up one of her bare feet and pointed. "You too!" Her face flushed with excitement.

"I don't think I will," he said, shaking his head. But he had stopped walking. The cool water sounded good. Heat swept over him. The expansive sky made his stomach feel empty and ravenous. Beads of sweat were starting to shine pink along his neck and temples. He tried to apologize with a smile—a flash of icy reddish gums.

Jo was determined. She leaned into each word of her appeal with her eyes locked on his. "Come on, Howard. No one's here. Just me. And all this. See, watch me." She gestured out at the water, that flawless glass, an inverted sky of rippling sheen. Stepping forward, tottering on the slippery stones, toes grasping the rock, she moved down into the water until it lapped above her ankles. She let out a shriek of cold and delight. "Howard!" She laughed and laughed, her chest light and her arms stretched out. "Get out here!" Her voice echoed across the cove.

She was like a child offering a flower in an outstretched hand, like a voice springing from a mountain. He could not keep himself from her offer. Something about the place, and her, left him helpless. He almost welcomed the surrender, the risk, the chance for someone else to see what he had become and in doing so render it real.

He unlaced his shoes and bent to tug them off, then the socks, freeing the livid red shock beneath the thin skin on the top of his feet. He braced himself for her revolted expression, but she wasn't even looking back at him. She walked further and further out into the water, stopping to pick up a stone from the bottom now and again, to turn it in her palm. By the time Howard rose and walked into the shallows—with a swell of pleasure at the water's chill on his bare skin—she was many yards ahead of him, nearly knee-deep, hands tapping her thighs with dripping fingers. She watched the horizon. She was her own tree, wave, and wind. The ebbing water had a cold grasp on her bones, but the pain was exquisite. She turned back to look at Howard. She yelled to him, victorious. "See, that's all right, isn't it?"

"It is," he said. He looked down at the river swirling around his ankles. Through the clear water, his toes looked skeletal, near white, covered by his clear skin and glassy nails. The workings of his foot, glaring crimson, created a reverse braid, as the large triple-cord of muscles unwound into long strands of muscle and tendon. Those mechanics attached to the base of each toe, wrapped in the fleshy gauze of fibrous sheaths. As Howard adjusted his balance, the flux of blood through the limb seemed like an illusion beneath the disturbance and regathering of the water's surface. The rock beneath created a blurry mosaic of broken gray, brown, and black.

Something large surfaced a few feet away from him. A large green-black something. A sound of awe was drawn from Jo's lips, and she pointed at it.

"I didn't see it," said Howard, just in time to see another churning of the water's surface a few feet beyond, the bend of a massive tail between himself and her. The huge fish rolled to its side, showing a brilliant lateral line, marked with a perfect string of diamonds twisting into a helix. The gray, lidless eye seemed to roll at the sky when it broke into the air. It shone like a bead, or a talisman. Jo jerked her arms up and squealed. She looked back at Howard with a thrilled, scared smile. A stunned laugh broke from him as she started rushing back toward the shore. But her calves were heavy and slow through the water compared to the fumbling rush of her upper body. Huge fins and curved, slick backs kept breaking the surface all around her. She almost slipped into the tumble of dark bodies. Howard reached her, up to his shins now, and held out his arms. He was strong enough to catch her from another stumble on an algae-slick rock, but just as quickly as they had held her up, the arms that Jo clung to shuddered and fell away. She sloshed onto her knees with a rush of icy cold as the water reached her hips.

A swift vibration sang through the air. Howard's pupils dilated and his head rolled forward, hair swaying as his legs crumpled beneath him. His body crashed into the river. There was a splash and sickening slap against the stones as his head hit the rock.

Jo screamed.

Howard's body shook violently, his limbs thrashing while the river washed away his painted face to reveal his bloody musculature in streaks. His round, rolling eyes stared through their streaked lids. His teeth parted in frantic gasps.

Jo screamed again.

"Howard! Oh my God. Oh my God, Howard! Shit! Oh, God." She moved with a strength and quickness fueled by terror. She grabbed his left arm and tugged with all her might, trying to right him up to a sitting position. Part of the skin at his lip had broken, and blood dripped into the water. Howard's body spun uselessly, his long limbs folding in all the wrong ways as Jo dragged him the few feet to the shore, pulling a deep furrow into the rocky riverbed as his weight scudded along the bottom.

Adrenaline surged as she hoisted his torso up to dry ground, the river still flowing over his shins and bare feet. Jo's knees slammed the rocky shore as she knelt to hold his gruesome head as still as she could. She choked on another scream. Tremors continued to course through Howard's body, and multiple new cuts sprung new blood. He was unconscious. She scrambled to her feet. Her wet, shaking hands grabbed for her cell phone inside the backpack. She tried to bring up the screen. No battery. Dead.

Jo put her hand to her mouth, thinking she was going to retch. She choked it back, turning her head, looking up the hill toward the cabin. She saw a flash of gray-blond hair—it had to be Sarah. "Hey! Wait!" Jo screamed, but Sarah was already retreating toward the dark cabin. Jo swore, looking down at Howard's bloody head.

She clawed a divot in the stones, shifting Howard's body, tipping his chin to the side. He was very still now, but still breathing. She didn't know what he was, what was wrong with him, but this much she knew—Howard needed an ambulance. Immediately.

Jo hurled her legs forward. She sprinted the barely worn path, cutting up the hill like a torrent. Wildflowers and shrubs stung her wet ankles. The cabin was just ahead, and she could now make out the familiar dented station wagon parked to the side of it. "Sarah?" Jo threw open the cabin door to find Sarah crouched over a set of cardboard boxes, drawing packing tape across their tops and pressing it smooth. Jo's words tumbled into the room as she burst into the kitchen, dripping wet, looking frantically for a telephone. "Sarah. It's me, Jo, look, I'm so sorry for this, but I—"

"This is my property. You're not supposed to be here." Sarah froze like something hunted. Her gaze seemed hollow. Jo felt wasted time rocketing past with every breath.

"A phone. Please, my friend collapsed! He's down at the river. We need to call an ambulance. He's—he looks bad. Really, really, bad. Please, can I use your phone?"

Sarah didn't move, did not seem to register the urgency of the situation. "My phone line is not connected right now," she said, looking to the left rather than at Jo. Her hands clutched at some crumpled paper on the kitchen table.

"He needs help now! I think he's dying!" Jo stormed toward Sarah. "Please, help me do something!" She grabbed both of Sarah's wrists and tugged her up to a standing position, managing to force her out the door.

Sarah wrenched her wrists, still held fast in Jo's hands, overhead and brought the heels of her hands down to strike Jo cleanly on her left cheekbone, hard. The blunted thud resulted in no cry from Jo, just her frantic face brought inches from Sarah's own.

Jo glared in fury. She was shaking from the shock of the blow, but her voice was compelling as a razorblade. "You need to see him," she said. She redoubled her grip on Sarah and tugged her downhill toward the water. Their footsteps nearly interlocked as Sarah struggled. But then, awakening to what she saw ahead of her, she stopped resisting and stared.

A man at the shoreline lay thin and helpless on his back, covered in sopping dark cloth. His feet, hands, and head might have been made with the stained flesh of cold weather chokecherries and deeply ripened plums, left skinned for feasting flies. Sarah had never seen anyone or anything like it. She melted into wonder. Seeing Sarah's change in expression, Jo loosened her grip. Sarah's hands fell to her sides. Both women rushed down to the water together.

Sarah knelt next to Howard. Her eyes swept over his exposed skin with sharp, frenetic movements. She hurled questions at Jo while she moved, alighting like a moth around Howard's body, pressing fingers to wrist to feel for a pulse, hovering ear over mouth to feel warm bursts of shallow breath.

"How long? How long has he been like this?"

"He fainted something like five minutes ago. But how long has he looked like this?" Jo bit her lip. "I have no idea." She was reframing every interaction she'd had with her neighbor as she rushed through the memories, the night in the rain when his face was exposed, the makeup she dismissed. Something was very wrong with this man. Terrifyingly wrong. She tried to look at him, but found she had to turn her head away.

Sarah reached for Jo's backpack, and deftly pulled Howard's legs over and up to elevate them, using the pack as support. "Do you know what his condition is? Does he have a diagnosis?"

"No! I don't know!" Jo said. She was pacing along the water's edge, trying to breathe through her tightened throat. "I don't even know him very well. He's my neighbor. He was shaking. His eyes rolled back before he fell. Sarah, he needs an ambulance!"

"No, no." Sarah's eyes flicked side to side. "We need to get him inside, warm, and stable. That's the most important thing." Her voice assumed a sense of forced command. "Go up to the house. Get two bedsheets from the closet across from the bedroom."

"Fuck." Jo complied, scrambling back up the hill as fast as she could.

Sarah looked down at Howard, letting her clinical eyes assess his form. There was an elegance to the corded lines that sketched his face—it was an absurd, grotesque beauty, the power of the body made transparent. So much more immediate than the anatomy diagrams she worked to memorize as an undergraduate student. Memories of her old lab came rushing back. Her white coat. Her forgotten, forsaken life. This man's wrists made her think of the glassy fish and frogs who used to swim in her tanks, showing light and dark organs through their slick, wet skin.

The bedsheets ballooned in the wind behind Jo as she rushed back down the hill. Sarah directed her, and together they spread and folded the fabric beside Howard, hauling him onto the improvised stretcher, first grasping underneath shoulders, then thighs, as carefully as possible, making sure his head was clear. Howard moaned quietly as they lifted, both women with shaking arm muscles pulling upward on the corners of the sheets. Howard was cradled, dragged, and swayed. Jo's grip loosened the further they climbed, and she twisted her elbow up, catching the sheet as it threatened to drop past her hip. Sarah's neck tensed with strain. Time seemed slow and thick as they approached the cabin. The door was left flung open, and warm air rushed in as they eased Howard down on the kitchen floor. Jo began crying, sobs breaking from her throat.

"Help me get him to the bed," Sarah said; and they did, with great effort, manage to carry him to the dark bedroom and heave him up to the undressed mattress. Jo stormed around the small room, rubbing her hands together, looking nervously at the boarded windows.

"OK, Sarah." Jo pressed both palms to her forehead. "You seriously don't have a phone? Why are the windows all boarded up? Jesus Christ."

"We need to get him warm, and I need to run a blood test," said Sarah.

"You need what? What are you talking about?"

Sarah looked disoriented. "I mean that he should have a blood test."

"At a hospital," finished Jo. She couldn't take it. She left the room, scouring the dark kitchen again for proof of a phone. Nothing. What would be useful? There was a red, gleaming man in the other room with an impossible sinew-and-bone face covered in blood. What could she do? She tore through boxes and cabinets, not even sure what she sought. She noticed the cardboard boxes half-packed with belongings. Was Sarah moving out? All seemed strange. The house was so dark. The peculiar light of the now-lowering sun crept in where it could. Jo noticed a cluster of medical equipment beside one of the piles of boxes—an IV that looked blemished from use, with a stiff, yellowed bag still attached. Jo mouthed a silent *what the hell?* She checked the upper cabinets. Empty. What she really needed to find was some liquor, a blessing, secreted away. Nothing in the upper cabinets. She kept looking.

In the bedroom, Howard convulsed with cold. Sarah started working to pull his arms out of their cold, wet sleeves, but they clung fast to his skin. She stepped out briskly, then was back in with scissors and a towel she'd extracted from a box in the hallway. The scissor blades cut clean, from the bottom seam of his shirt's black jersey cotton all the way up to the throat of the turtleneck. As the fabric peeled back, Sarah saw the dark violet coil of his organs between the lapses in the screen of red muscle. Howard's jaw tilted upward as she wiped his chest, the motion tender, maternal. She placed her hand against the cool flesh of his chest, stunned with wonder at the localized bloom of his heartbeat, visible as a pumping surge of crimson that edged to the right of his sternum and through the pectorals. The shape of his chest barely caged the ever-bursting red. Beat. Bloom. Beat. Bloom. Sarah knew about cells and bodies, but this was like the work of an artist's hand. He was otherworldly. And then he was looking up at her, eyes careening to finally find her face.

"Who are you?" he asked. His voice was quiet as a lover's. "Please. Please, no one should see me. Nobody can know about me. Please. No pictures. No tests." She couldn't respond. She had too many emotions to name. He tried to roll to the side, away from her, but she pressed his shoulder down, holding him easily onto the bed. She placed pillows under his legs to elevate them. The bone white of his brow coiled up in her awareness and his open eyes were locked on her face. The space of years dissipated, and she felt the old problems absorb her: the quandary of the misfiring human body, the lure of divining a cure, the gaping need for solution. It was all alive and breathing, right here before her.

"I'm no one," she told him, covering his bare torso with a sheet and a brown army surplus blanket that she took from the top shelf in the otherwise empty closet. "But I used to be someone different."

Howard nodded, clear eyelids drooping, and lost consciousness again.

Sarah knew that it was possible that he might never wake up. It was more and more possible the longer she stood still. Memories swarmed her. The name she used to sign at the bottoms of forms. Sharps-disposal containers. Latex gloves. The study in guilt she had become. Sarah's cold eyes met Jo's dark, inkblot ones as the younger woman reappeared in the hallway. Sarah couldn't stop her words—they just tumbled out. "The neighbors a few miles to the south will have a phone. It's just ... I'm moving, and my mobile minutes are all used up. Prepaid." She looked down, then to Howard, still out cold, and back at Jo. "I know what to do to keep him stable. Will you go?" She drew a set of keys from her left pocket.

Jo whispered, "Thank you," grabbed the keys, and rushed out.

32

JO HURRIEDLY BUCKLED HERSELF INTO the driver's seat of the old station wagon, struggling with the twisted seat belt strap. She started the vehicle. On the passenger seat, she noticed an envelope that had papers tucked inside. Jo cranked the car into reverse and pivoted out of the gravel drive. She shot down the road with the waning sun shining brightly into the side of her right eye. One mile clicked past on the odometer, then another. She craned her neck, looking for any sign of the house Sarah had mentioned, but she saw nothing, just the road and trees and more trees.

She wondered if she should turn around to get on the highway. There had to be a driveway soon, a mailbox, something. Where the hell was it? Did she miss something obvious in her panic? But then she spotted a cluster of red and blue birdhouses at the mouth of an opening in the woods. An address placard stood just behind them. She turned in. At the end of a winding driveway, Jo found a cottage that was meticulously maintained, blue with white trim. She threw the gear into park.

She was out of the car, over the paver stones, up to the door. She knocked and rang the doorbell multiple times. Nobody answered. Jo swore.

She turned and thought to get back in the station wagon but wheeled back around and knocked frantically one more time. Still no answer, but then she thought she heard laughter. She ran around to the back of the house, where she found a man and a woman, both sporting buzz cuts, sitting in folding chairs on their deck. They were eating baked beans and burgers off paper plates.

Jo ran onto the deck, looking utterly insane. The woman jerked up from her chair in surprise, spilling the beer from her can into her lap. The man let out a small, startled grunt, and then laughed.

"Whoa, Marta. Easy there," he said to his wife, reaching for a napkin off a pile kept from the wind by a rock that sat on top. He addressed Jo with a smirk. "What in the name of Sam Hill are you doing here on my property, young lady? You look like you seen something in the woods." The lines at the edges of his eyes crinkled with good humor. He set his paper plate down on the deck.

Jo shook her head. "Please, it's an emergency. I tried to knock, but—look, can I use a cell phone? My friend is hurt, up the road. It's very urgent." Marta was already fishing her cell phone from the pocket of her beer-soaked khaki shorts and handing it to Jo with a muttered "Goddamn."

The man was saying something like "She just came out of nowhere, didn't she?" as Jo pressed the three numbers. What would she say? She hadn't rehearsed this part in her mind. The dispatcher answered. Marta mopped her shorts with a second and third napkin.

"Hello! I need to report a medical emergency—" She turned to the couple to ask their address, which she repeated. "He's a couple miles up from here, Moss Falls? No, I don't know the address. Yes, it's off 61. There's no phone at the residence. No. Yes, an ambulance. Please just come quickly. It's the next driveway to the north. He's maybe in his thirties? Yes, he's breathing. No, not conscious. Uh, he looks really bad. I can't describe it. Yes, his name is Howard. No, I don't know his last name. No, I can't stay on the line, I'm sorry." She hung up.

Jo was shaking, hoping she said the right things. Her cheeks were streaked with tears that kept coming. She handed the cell phone back to Marta.

"Joe," said the man, sticking his hand out to shake hers.

"Me too," she said, rubbing her tears away with the back of her hand. "Jo, I mean. It's my name, too." Both of them smiled at her. Joe cracked open a new can of beer and held it out to her.

"You might need a couple swigs. Take the edge off." Jo looked at him gratefully and tipped the can back like a salvation. The couple walked with her out to the driveway, watching the darkening road for red lights. They stood straight-backed in the odd easy quiet of strangers waiting for something together. Jo could feel her heart unmooring, in the yard fettered with birdfeeders and garden ornaments, with the faint smoke of the smoldering firepit behind the house, with Marta reaching for her husband's hand when he cleared his throat, and she let herself long for her family. The simple presence of this couple shook something loose. How long had it been since she'd called her parents? What on earth made her think she could belong here in this wild place?

Even so far from the city, the ambulance sirens came sooner than Jo thought they would. She ran to the curb, pointing wildly, urging them further along the road as they flew north. She didn't know if they saw her or not. As the sound faded, Marta ran her hands over the back of her head and asked if Jo would like to come inside and stay awhile. Jo shook her head. "Is there someone else we could call for you?" asked Joe. "We want to make sure you're all right." A line wrinkled into the center of his forehead. She wanted to say yes, let this older couple offer her blankets and peace and a sleep uninterrupted by terror, but she couldn't. Her cat, sweet Ike, hadn't been fed yet today. Taking care of him was something she could do. The thought of his warm furry body sitting by the door, waiting patiently for her, made her eyes well up again.

Jo touched his arm in thanks and nodded at Marta. "Thank you so much for everything, but I don't think I can intrude any more than I already have."

"Suit yourself. We've always got a cold beer if you ever need one." He and Marta waved and walked back around the house to the deck, no doubt to finish the last half of their cookout dinner, now gone cold, and to speculate about their unexpected visitor.

Jo got back into the station wagon, feeling the way her pulse seemed both too slow and too loud all at once. She took stock of her situation. Was her backpack still near the shore? Her phone? Her camera? She put the key in the ignition and turned, but the car idled in the driveway for a full ten minutes before Jo swallowed and finally found herself steady enough to put it in reverse.

33

THE SCREAM OF THE SIRENS made its way to the gravel drive in front of Sarah's cabin. Moments later, three men leapt out of the ambulance and rushed toward the door, ready to respond. As he ran, the senior paramedic thought how easy it would have been to miss seeing this residence. It was so small, and so entrenched in overgrown bushes and brush that it almost looked like it was being consumed by the forest, especially in the dying light.

"Hello?"

The paramedics found the door unlocked, swinging open easily when they pushed it in, but the place was all dark. One man yanked the cord for the kitchen light. Cabinets were ajar. There was no sign of anyone, just piles of cardboard boxes. The team rushed through the small house. Everything was dark—were the windows boarded? It was strange. It looked like no one had entered the cabin in months. The bed was stripped, the place nearly empty, but there was fresh water and dirt tracked on the floors. They called out, boots trudging through the small rooms again and again. "Anyone here? We are responding to a call about a medical emergency." No answer. One man opened closet doors while another ran outside, circling the house, looking and listening for any signs of distress. He heard the slow lapping of the river and the evening cries of birds, nothing else.

"Radio dispatch," he yelled out front to his partners. "Ask them again about the location." He shined his flashlight around the yard, saw nothing. His strong legs pushed through the tall grass.

The lights on the parked ambulance were still whirling red and yellow. "Do you think it's the wrong place?" They reasoned that it must be. There wasn't a sure location from the caller, who had dropped off the line after the initial contact. The place looked abandoned; it all felt wrong. They exchanged concerned glances.

Precious seconds were ticking by. They heard another siren wailing to the north. More responders, probably county police. This wasn't right. They notified dispatch that they were unable to make contact at the first residence, and that they would keep looking further up the road. Someone, somewhere, was running out of time, and they had wasted too much of it already. The ambulance started up the road again and picked up speed.

ALONG THE SIDE of the cabin, buried under a thick mat of old, vining brush—other than what Sarah had torn away in rapid fistfuls—the wide old wooden doors of a root cellar were closed against the night. Howard had struggled for air, his breath coming in rattling gulps, as he staggered out of the house, blanket pulled tight around his shoulders, with most of his weight supported by Sarah. He had just enough strength to lower himself down into the hole. Sarah had crawled in afterward and shut the doors above them.

Now he crouched on the dirt floor of the cellar, bathed in darkness. Sarah was curled up in the remaining space. Her hands were pressing into the soil. Her eyes were shut fast. She tried to smother the small sounds of her fear as she heard the ambulance arrive, the voices. She grasped Howard's hand. The men shouted to each other, but soon they were gone.

As they heard the siren fade back into the distance, Sarah felt Howard's hand relax and heard his breath come easier. He tipped his chin toward her, even though he knew she, like him, could see nothing but blackness and the deep violet line where the starlight cracked through the gap in the old cellar doors above.

"Thank you," he whispered. She put a hand on his back.

Sheltered in earth, below the ground, the two stayed still, feeling their veins turn to root systems, their faces to leaves. There was no need to speak. No one could find them and the fact of that was comforting enough that both lost themselves to sleep as the night went on, each leaning against their own wall of cool earth.

WHEN JO MADE the wide turn into the gravel drive, she remembered the envelope and documents in the passenger seat. She guessed that Sarah might have forgotten to take them in. They looked important. Jo grabbed them and jogged to the door. But she found the cabin complete-ly dark, the door unlocked, the rooms empty.

"Sarah?" Jo called into the dark, tossing the envelope and Sarah's keys on the table. Had the ambulance already taken Howard, and Sarah along with him? She turned on the light, and a pair of mosquitos lilted in circles around the bulb. Jo rushed through each small room. No one. She checked each a second time to make certain, but the cabin was vacant. The blankets on the bed where she had last seen Howard were gone. They must have taken him, then, she thought. So fast. She wondered if she should wait for Sarah to return. But the evening wind careened through the small cabin in such a lonely way. Back in the kitchen, she saw the keys to Howard's truck sitting with purpose on the kitchen table. Sarah must have found them in his pocket. Were they meant for her? She convinced herself he would want her to take his truck back home. The surreal dissonance of the night's events was beginning to rattle her adrenaline-exhausted body. She ached to get home.

She could do it. Back through the woods—it wasn't far. She'd get her camera, take Howard's truck back to its parking space, feed the cat and sleep off this whole thing. He had her email address and phone number; of course he would get in touch with her when he was home. She had to take care of herself now. All she needed to do was get back through the trail.

She rummaged around in the front closet, quickly finding a heavy-duty camping flashlight standing on end toward the back of a bottom shelf. She grabbed it, clicked it on and off; the flashlight looked ancient, but the beam was strong. She thought about leaving a note for Sarah but thought better of it. Sarah would figure it out. Time to go. Remembering the cash for Sarah wadded up in the pocket of her shorts—yes, it was still there—Jo left it on the table, an offering that now seemed like something from another life.

With the flashlight piercing the night in front of her, Jo walked out of the house and down the hill to the water. There, she picked up her strewn-about pack, and found her camera intact. The casing was cold and damp from condensation, but it seemed unharmed. She twisted the lens out of habit, adjusting focus in and out, in and out. Turning the power to ON, she saw the message SUBJECT IS TOO DARK flashing. She clutched the camera close in relief. It was functioning. She placed it in the pack with her other things. Her phone was there, but still dead as ever; she prayed she'd be able to find her way back to the highway entrance in the dark without navigation.

The wind was restless. Water lapped at the shore. The sounds followed her as Jo went back down through the wooded path, spearing the light of the flashlight always ahead. She walked as quickly as she dared. Every shadow held a space for sleeping creatures and their wet, red, waiting mouths. She picked her way over roots and rocks. She stumbled once into the brush, cursing. She feared the shifting darkness.

There was the slow slide of something moving against the branches to the side of her, or behind her, a wet rustle that froze her in place.

She felt the sting of cuts and dirt on her bare legs. Everything was echoing inside her, banging against her chest: the burn in her throat, the way she had tried to hold Howard's head still as his body shook in the river, the man who looked dead but was not, and now, the forest night compressing itself around her. Closer. Heavier. She remembered what Howard had said, in the truck. The shipwrecks. The ghosts.

In the madness of fear, she hugged the flashlight against her body, took three quick breaths, and turned it off. She closed her eyes, staying as still as she could. If she'd looked behind her, she'd have seen the white glow of the sailor, still holding his doused lantern by its handle. If she turned around, would he stop, looking embarrassed in his eternal youth, and ask after his wife—was she well? Was she worried? Jo felt a soft push against her back, a whisper against her neck.

Oh, my darling, she thought, but it was someone else's thought.

She gasped. At the sound, the young man, with his century-old shirt still wet on his incorporeal form, was frightened into elsewhere. Jo felt the leaving, though she didn't know what it was. The air got warmer.

She turned the flashlight on and began walking forward, forward until, mercifully, she saw the woods open to the sight of Howard's green Ford pickup. Still there waiting for her.

It was only once she was back behind the steering wheel that she started to sob again, in wonder and relief, heading south toward Duluth.

34

IN THE DAYS THAT FOLLOWED, Jo went to work as scheduled, did her job, and said nothing about the night at Moss Falls. Howard's truck stayed in its old parking spot where she'd parked it. After a week passed, she dropped Howard's keys off at the office along with her rent. She left a note attached to forward the keys to the tenant in unit 13. As for herself, she hadn't seen him.

Whenever she was home and heard footsteps coming down the hallway, usually splashing her drink over the edge of her glass in her rush, she would run to the door and press her eye to the peephole. But it was never him. She had to assume that the hospital would have notified his family about what happened. No one new seemed to have moved in, so she hoped Howard might be still sending his rent from wherever he was recovering. She wanted to write him by email again, but she ended up deleting every letter she started.

She didn't really know him anyway, she reasoned. It was better to start setting her mind hard on forgetting all of it.

The months drew on, summer warmed in earnest, and she continued to work, drink, and wonder what was next. She didn't go out. She started talking to her parents more on the phone. She knew they worried about her. They said she could come back home.

When she slept, though, Jo's subconscious still wouldn't let Howard slip away. One night, she dreamed she was back in Sarah's cabin, spreading a blanket over his brilliantly beating chest. The felt was thin, brown, pilled. Threadbare as the blanket was, it looked so thick compared to Howard's exposed skin, translucent and amphibious. It stayed wet-looking even as she tried to brush it dry several times with the corner of the blanket. He looked at her. He looked so cold. A breathing, bleeding body in such a thin shell. A horror. His hand reached for hers, but she didn't take it. He was saying something, his voice all spectral lightness, but she couldn't understand. She longed to say something back, but each time found herself voiceless.

In the morning, she still felt cold when she swallowed. She didn't have normal days anymore. She knew that she had traded a sense of normalcy for something else. What it was, she didn't know, but she felt its presence, like she had gained some kind of risk or rarity that was part of her blood now.

"TAKE THIS ONE with you," Tonya told her at the end of her last workday at Trenton Floral. The season was ending, and Jo's position would not be extended through the fall. Tonya thrust a remarkable white rose with wide-open petals at Jo. It was wrapped loosely in brown paper and twine. The flower was perfect: too open to sell, but at the peak of its outstretched beauty. They had spent a long Saturday packing up the greenhouse. "I hope you'll think about coming back next year," Tonya said. Jo nodded, feeling an empty sense of sureness, and left.

The rose now sat on Jo's counter, where she was lining up the bottles of liquor she had left, all of them nearing empty, since she'd promised herself, again, not to buy any more. She started with the shortest, then up to the tallest. She turned each one so that the flat planes touched, or the point of a curve met with a corner. Lamplight radiated through the glass shapes. The blurry room was magnified behind them. She unwrapped the rose from its paper. Touching the petals to her lips, she marveled at the softness, the curl. She twisted open the last bottle in the line and guided the stem of the rose down through the throat of the bottle until it was stem-deep in two inches of whiskey. The rose would wilt, she knew. Then again, it was dead already.

Jo picked up her phone and dialed Cait. She picked up after two rings.

"Hey," Jo said, voice breaking. "I need you."

35

CAIT ARRIVED AT JO'S DOOR in her sweats, with her red hair askew.
When Jo let her in, her face was alight with worry. She looked around
the apartment, took in the empty whiskey bottles, the pile of unopened
mail on the counter, the sleeping cat in the corner, and her friend, looking so small, on the couch with a quilt around her shoulders. Jo shrugged
through her tears. Cait sat down next to her, opening arms to hold her
close. She had only texted with Jo throughout the busy summer. She
knew Jo's job had just ended. She wondered how many other things she
didn't know.

"There's nothing else lined up?" asked Cait, once Jo's tears started to
slowly dry up. Used tissues mounded on the floor between them.

"No, I know I should have been on that, but I really thought Trenton might keep me on. I don't know how I'm going to pay for anything,
and I'm really fighting with my drinking. I feel like I haven't gained any
ground." She tossed another tissue onto the pile.

"Oh, Josephine." Cait brushed Jo's dark hair back from where it
stuck to her forehead. She swore at herself for not knowing that things
had gotten this bad for her friend. "You are carrying way too much,"
she said. "It hasn't even been a year since you and Josh split." Jo nodded
silently. Cait sighed. "I'm sorry, I didn't know it was like this. I should've
fucking been here for you."

"I should have asked. I thought I could do all this on my own. God, I don't know if I should even be in this city."

"Listen," said Cait, pointing to her black duffel bag left by the door. "I brought all my stuff to stay the night on your couch. I have Rachel running the café tomorrow. Right now, I want you to just worry about getting to sleep, and then tomorrow, I'm going to take you to see some sights. We're going to help you reset. We're going to have a whole day together to figure this all out. I'm here, OK?"

"What did I ever do to deserve you?" asked Jo, gratitude flooding her entire posture. Cait shook her head and yawned. Jo put her hand to her mouth, echoing the yawn. "Hang on though. Before we try to get some sleep, can I show you something? I meant to send you these months ago."

"Of course."

Jo rose and fetched her camera from under the bed. She flipped it on and sat back down on the couch next to Cait. "Remember how you said I should go up the shore? Back in May?"

"Yeah, I do. You did it after all?"

Jo nodded. As she switched the camera mode to view, the preview screen lit up with the fullness of water and a luminous late afternoon sky. Cait gasped. She looked at Jo and started clicking back through the images, folds of leaves, the muted grays and browns of the wild north, the textures of bark and rock. Then, she came to a photograph of trees framing a woodland trail, arced like a living cathedral ceiling. A tall, dark figure stood framed in the distance beneath them, backlit by the sun, in the perfect center of the composition. The humidity of the air had fogged the lens, so the man was little more than a hazy silhouette, a graceful bend to his spine as he looked up into the mist.

"Who is this?" asked Cait, pointing at the screen and looking at her friend with wide eyes.

"A guy who used to live next door."

"Used to?"

"Yeah."

Cait raised her eyebrows and tilted her head.

"Anything else?"

Jo took the camera back from Cait's gentle hands. "No," she said. She wet her lips. "No. Not really."

36

JO AWOKE TO THE AROMA of coffee, and the sight of Cait, with her red hair spilling over her shoulders, handing her a mug. She took the offering and shuffled sleepily out. At the kitchen table, Jo started opening bills and making a list. Cait watched her and petted the meowing Ike absentmindedly. Jo's hand clutched her pen with a tension that ran all the way up to her shoulder. When she'd tipped the last hot drip of coffee back, Cait took the mug, along with her own, to the sink and started tackling the dishes. She plunged her hands into the hot suds while Jo moved paper into piles.

"Are you ready for an adventure today?" Cait asked, flipping the drying towel over her shoulder. Jo looked out the window dubiously at the graying sky.

"Looks like rain."

Cait shook her head. "Where I'm taking you, that won't matter."

THEY WALKED INTO the spacious atrium of the Great Lakes Aquarium to the echoing sound of children's voices, the hum of machines keeping filters running, and streams of air bubbling through aerated tanks. Jo stayed close to Cait, who knew her way around. After getting their tickets, they rode the escalator upward to the main floor. Speakers pumped out recorded sounds of Minnesota birds and distant thunder. Soon they were winding through walls of tanks and lush displays.

Together they pointed, took pictures, brought their faces up to glass in the living galleries highlighting the animals of the Great Lakes region. There was a tumbling manmade waterfall that made Jo think of Moss Falls. Trout drifted happily against the current as the water spilled down. Jo stared at them until her eyes went glassy. Families with kids passed in front and behind, but Jo didn't step aside. Cait noticed but waited for her to say something.

"This just reminds me of how much beauty this place has, everything around here, up north. I understand why people move here."

"People?" Cait asked. "Not you?"

Jo put a hand against the glass, watching the scales of the trout glittering beneath. "I think I need to move back to Iowa." Outside, a storm was coming in over the lake, visible across the room through the tall glass wall looking out over Lake Superior. "I thought I could be one of those people who could make her own life. Someone who can put gear in a canoe and go out on her own. Had some fantasy about exploring the Boundary Waters. But look at me. I'm not making it. There are people who love me, who want to help me through. I need to stop pretending I don't need that." She rubbed her forehead. "Why would someone choose to be alone when they didn't have to be?"

"Is your rent month-to-month?"

"Yeah. It will be easy enough. But I feel like a wreck for coming this far, making this whole big move, just to fail. To go home. What have I gained?"

Cait slipped her arm around Jo's waist and squeezed. "The North works on all of us in strange ways. You might just not know how it worked on you yet. It's not a waste. There are lakes in Iowa, too."

Jo nodded. Cait saw an otter playing with a ball in the next display and started to laugh, pulling Jo into her joy. There was so much to see.

Seahorses grasped aquatic plants with their delicate tails. A rescue eagle stretched his thick wings.

They walked through the dim green light of an exhibit on invasive species and found themselves in front of a stunning two-story, 85,000-gallon tank swirling with fish native to Isle Royale. Jo looked closer and noticed the monstrous beings along the bottom, their bare white bellies, their dark plated scales, their mouths extending.

"Those fish! What are those? What—" Jo asked, her excitement barely contained. A young aquarium guide with curly brown hair was in earshot and stepped up beside them. She had an enthusiastic smile and a sturgeon sticker on her plastic name tag.

"Those are our lake sturgeon!" she said, happy to launch into her educator speech. "They are the largest freshwater fish in the Great Lakes. Pretty incredible, aren't they?" She gestured Jo and Cait forward, into a part of the tank that curved inward for up-close viewing. Surrounded by the concave of glass, it felt like they were underwater. The sturgeon, each one easily bigger than Jo, dwarfed the other fish, and eyed the three women with lazy, dragonlike expressions.

Jo pointed at the biggest one as it drifted by, almost shaking. "I think I saw some of these, in a river. It was earlier this spring, around the middle of May."

"Really?" asked Cait, shooting an incredulous glance at Jo.

"Wow, sounds like you were really lucky!" The guide seemed overjoyed. "Sturgeon usually live in the deeper parts of the lake, but once a year they do migrate upriver to spawn. They always return to the same place, the river where they were born, even many years later. They have a very long lifespan. That's why they get so big."

Jo thought about that, and she lost herself in the motion of the gigantic fish drifting around the tank. The guide and Cait were on either side of her, silently delighting in the fish flying around and above them in their world of water and glass. Jo turned to the guide. "So, how do they know it's time to find their way home again?"

The guide watched as a large sturgeon turned just before the glass. "Some of it's the water levels and the temperature. But mostly, they just know."

37

EVELYN CALLED HER SON HOWARD on the phone for the third time that afternoon. No answer. What had started as annoyance began to turn to fear. Howard usually answered when she had sent a new check. It was the tithe she paid to maintain the thin veneer of a relationship with him. Of course, she knew she didn't deserve as much, but it was something. After Howard's father Edward died all those years ago, she lost the part of her that felt like a mother. Her nights were too haunted, too consumed with sorrow. She remembered the snow that night, the way the space underneath her husband's eyes flinched when he said he was going out for a drive. There were ways in which Howard still reminded her of him.

Things weren't perfect between them in their marriage, but Lord, how she had loved that man. Even with his difficult and taciturn manner. And the secret about his brother, Sam, which also became hers to keep. That secret stalked their property, the just-woken vestige of a nightmare.

He lived on the edge of their land, the same land where they poured tea, fought quietly, grew vegetables, and raised a son. Sam never spoke to her. She only saw him in lingering glimpses when she happened to be in the yard at the wrong time.

While Sam would gently take her charity, the leftover roast set out on the back porch, the bundles of fruit set out in the cold, he wasn't living a real life. It was the life of a wild man, a myth, a feral and stolen thing that they all worked to hide from the child.

Sam never knew Howard as his nephew, never saw him other than from a long distance. He understood why it had to be that way. He was careful to stay hidden. He came around to the yard less and less as the years marched on, sometimes going months without speaking, even to Edward. When young Howard spotted him one evening around sunset, a red flash of a bloody man in the woods, the child's insistence on what he had seen concerned Evelyn. But how they had worked to convince the boy that it wasn't real—she often worried about the impact that had, wondered whether it had been the right thing to do. Not only was the wild man real, but he was their own flesh and blood. A beloved brother who had so often been alone, but now lived his withdrawn, wandering life like a vow. It was Edward's promise, not hers, to look after him. She imagined she could hear Sam's weeping every time she neared the woods at the back of the lot to cut the wild brush back. Above all, she did everything she could to discourage Howard's fears of the bloody monster he kept insisting he saw. It was her way of making things more like the way they should've been.

And then, to have Edward rush home from work that night, only to head out into the snowdrifts after a harsh word from her. He knew the roads. He should've known it wasn't safe to drive, but an ice-slick turn slid him swift to his death. It was too much. Why hadn't she instead put a hand to his dark beard? Why hadn't she told him of the way she lost her mind with longing for him when he went silent?

She became so lonely after that.

Most of the time when she looked at her son, though he couldn't have known it, she was watching his skin for signs of betrayal. She became so distant that they hardly spoke. She provided for Howard, of course, just as she continued to sneak food left over from dinner onto the back porch that would disappear overnight. But as the years passed,

Evelyn lost her son as much as she had lost his father, and it was because she had dropped the tether between them, too weak and too tired to hold on to it.

She didn't try to stop her son from going to college, or from settling in a different state. She didn't pretend that there was much between them to hold onto as he entered his adult years. The money she sent to Howard, the phone calls, those were her way of casting the tether toward him again, trying. He took the end up, as a formality, as a tribute to the title Mother, but dropped it again each time as soon as they hung up. She liked to sit on the porch when she called him, to look across the huge wild field she'd let rise in place of yard, and stare into the trees. It had been years since she'd seen any sign of Sam. Perhaps he had died or moved on. All her offerings went untouched.

She was ashamed to admit that these more recent, quiet years, she had wished for his face at her door. Could she take warmth from the mouth of a monster? She didn't know. But what happened to all of them was beyond her capacity to process. She remembered Howard watching her face at his father's funeral. She knew she assigned the blame to her, though he may not have known what to call it.

But now, the emails unanswered, the phone left to ring—Evelyn was poor at being a mother, yes, but she did know her son. He hardly left his apartment.

She hoped she was wrong, but she couldn't help but imagine a dooming stained-glass pane of red superimposed over Howard's graceful face. The genetic inheritance she had always prayed would not be his.

Evelyn suddenly wished very much that she would have told Howard the truth a long time ago. She logged onto her bank account to see if the check she sent had been cashed. He should have gotten it weeks ago, but there was no sign of a withdrawal.

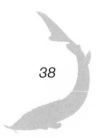

38

THAT AUTUMN, A WHISPER SPREAD from one hiker to another, to seven, to thirty, until anybody who walked the Lake Superior Trail was bound to hear about it. They talked in low tones about seeing the bloody man—a ghostly figure that walked the more remote parts of the North Shore. Some said he was an accident victim who had never realized his own death. Others insisted he was a mentally unstable vagrant who painted himself red to try to scare people away. Shortly after the first rumors sparked, little groups started organizing meetups to talk about whether he was real or not. They broke down hoaxes, speculated about his range and origin, and planned out the best ways to try for their own spotting.

In the upper level of a coffeehouse in Grand Marais, five people squeezed in together on the wraparound bench surrounding the corner table. One woman had a notebook with her, making stars along the page as she shared her theory inspired by the folklore of the Coos tribe in the Pacific Northwest. "They believe that forest spirits come in different forms," she said, slurping her mocha. "They can be ghosts that reanimate corpses—that seems to fit. Or they can be reflections of ourselves. Or just these giant beings that live off fish."

A young man in a flannel shirt shook his head. "I call bullshit," he said, raising his voice above the rumbling noise of the coffee grinder. "I could go into the woods, paint my skin red, and just eat fish all the time without being supernatural."

His buddy punched him on the arm, "You know the woods changes you, though. If you're in there for long enough, something happens. These people knew stuff, man, centuries ago. I'm telling you, they would know exactly what this is."

"That's what I'm saying," said the woman with the notebook. "There's something old out there. Always has been. Otherwise, where did all those old myths come from in the first place?"

"Do you really think he's human, or like a Sasquatch or something?" asked a tall teenager with long black hair. She swirled her straw around in her icy whipped drink. They debated and theorized until the last remaining barista loudly clacked the sign on the door from OPEN to CLOSED and cleared her throat pointedly. The group returned to their vehicles and drove home, wondering about the world and everything in it that couldn't quite be explained.

Over the next several years, a reported sighting would occasionally hit the local newspaper or somebody's social media page, but nobody ever managed to get a convincing photograph. While the particulars of the stories fluctuated, they all seemed to agree on one aspect of the bloody man—the second he saw that you were there, he'd take off running like a bat out of hell. He was more scared of you than you were of him, like so many other wild things that lived in the forest.

A SHADOW LEANED over the water. The fish could see it from the deeper bottom beyond the ledge. It was an uncertain and spindly dark shape, but the fish was untroubled by what loomed above. With a swish of his powerful spine, he was off in search of something he could eat. The owner of the shadow smiled at the sun and the cooling air. Above the water, there was nobody around. Just the quiet rustle of trees, and just a man whose muscles and blood shone through his face like a bowl of red berries shedding their juice. He moved in a half-limping way but without pain. He knew one soul he could trust and that was enough. He was building a small, simple shelter further inland, but for now he knew he was secret enough, learning to become a forager and hunter. Something like a monster of the woods. And if he ever saw a person, he could hide. He could run. Unless, of course, if the person was Jo.

If she ever came back, he would write her the poetry that he imagined when he looked at the earth. He would make a bed of branches and they would sleep in each other's arms. They would watch the moon together. He was stilled at the thought. He felt a small wintry chill become insistent beneath the fall breeze.

Beneath it all, he knew he would never see her again.

But it was nice to think about. It was nice to live.

39

JO ARRIVED AT THE Duluth Transit Center with a duffel strap crossed over each shoulder, a backpack behind that, and a cat carrier hooked over one arm. The Greyhound bus arrived, the sound of its brake escaping like a sigh and a shriek. It would take her south far before the chill of winter hit, to warm arms that were waiting to care for her. Still, she looked back and wondered what the North would have made of her. She had to leave before it got all the way into her lungs. An efficient, brusque worker loaded her luggage. The gray cat Ike would ride in his carrier. She murmured to him not to be afraid of the bus. He flicked his tail and mewed.

Jo settled herself into a window seat in an empty row, securing Ike's carrier in the open seat next to her. The other passengers spaced themselves out, donning headphones, opening newspapers, and powering up their tablet screens after fastening their seatbelts. They departed, and Jo let the drum of the wheels along the road resonate through her bones.

She checked the calendar on her phone. Just a week until the final divorce hearing. The thought felt so far from her. That would be it, next Tuesday—the last time she'd be in the same room with Joshua. She knew it would hurt to look at him. But she was ready now, for finality, this cord to sever and others to mend. She was bringing everything inside of her that had escaped back home—all those things that were wilder, that had tried to stand but couldn't yet, all the starved things she had found and loved enough to save.

She ran her hand through her dark hair, short as ever, just like she liked it. She wiggled her fingers, admiring the shimmer of her bright blue fingernails that Cait had painted for her the night before in exchange for a promise to come back to visit soon. She peered into the carrier to check on Ike, who had curled himself into a wheel and was already snoozing contentedly. She texted her projected arrival time to her parents and dug into her backpack to find the novel she'd been meaning to start reading for so long. Her hand seized the abused paperback shoved along the side and tugged it out. An erratically folded piece of paper was caught between the back cover and the final page. Curious, Jo unfolded it and turned it over. It was a familiar photocopied map. She smoothed the creases down as she spread the paper over her lap. Tracing the circle around Moss Falls with her ring finger, there was the lightest ache inside of her. But it was just the shadow of her own image, captured in a Polaroid photograph, collecting dust in an empty apartment back in Duluth, come to say goodbye.

She folded the map and tucked it back toward the later chapters. She opened the cover and started to read the first page of her book, then another and another and another as the landscape whipped by.

The hours stretched ahead, and the bus tilted to true south, now moving parallel to the Mississippi's flow down between state lines. Jo pictured herself holding a wooden paddle dripping with water, disrupting a smooth reflection of sky. She felt like she could smell home the minute they crossed into Iowa, all corn husks, dust, and the lemony leaves of linden trees.

40

ON THE MORNING OF THE first snow, Sarah woke and started preparing for her friend's arrival. She set a kettle to boil and started organizing dried jerky, fresh vegetables, and nutrition bars into containers. He preferred to stay out on the trail for a full week at a time these days. He was accustomed to it now. While she waited for his return, she enjoyed working on things to fortify him. He never asked for much, but she kept lemonade in the refrigerator, put together nonperishable meal kits, and thrifted new warm clothes for him when she could. She never knew right when he would show up, only that he would.

He was a medical marvel, and she worked out ways to care for him. He offered up whatever he could of use—his social security number, his small income from writing when he could sit still long enough to do it. Sometimes, she'd stop in a restaurant on her way to Ahlborn's to upload his work on a secondhand laptop. For the price of a hot mug of black coffee, she'd have time at a table to manage his accounts. She was able to help him monitor his body and theorize about what was happening inside of it. She had expected more seizures for him, but none more had come, at least not that he ever told her about. His gait was halting, but he moved along just fine. In fact, as far as she knew, he rarely stopped walking. That seemed to be the only thing that ailed him, other than his skin's lost pigmentation. She never sent his blood in for a test, never verified anything more about his genes than what she could surmise with the data she had. Her scientific curiosity busied itself around his condition, but her truest longing was simply to be left alone and forgotten. His wish for the same comforted her. It cemented her devotion. The two never touched, but moved easily in the same space, awakening a warmth and steadiness that Sarah couldn't remember having felt before. It was enough.

He appeared on that early winter morning looking nothing less than a voyageur, wearing an old, worn fur-lined coat and thick breeches. He pushed the hood off his head with mittened hands as he stepped through the doorway, the first snow crystals glimmering in the sunlit air. A joyful grimace of a smile tore across the face of red and bone. He was something remarkable. His flesh resembled both the twitching flank of a freshly skinned fish and the bisected phloem of a tree trunk, sweet with sap. Now, in his thick coat, he seemed almost like the gatekeeper of the dark winter woods. He could have been a sentinel of death. He could have been a lord of the lake. But he was just a quiet man, living as a shadow among the trees, who spent a certain number of colder nights on her couch, always folding the blankets back up neatly before he left.

"You know I can't cure you," she said, "Even though maybe I could have once." Each time, she began with that.

"I keep waiting to die," he said, "but you know, I don't think I'm going to." Sarah wiped at the counter with a faded gray towel. His eyes were far away. "I was just watching the water a few miles up, along the bank. Anything could be beneath that surface, and we would never know."

Sarah smirked.

"I mean, really," he said, "No idea. Nobody has any idea about anything." She shook her head.

"There's an answer for it all," she said. "It's just not always what we think it will be. Doesn't come how we think it will. Belief, environment, they both shape us."

Howard eased his thin form into one of the metal folding chairs at the table, snowflakes turning to droplets on the fur of his hood. His hair had grown longer, though the beard was still only a sketch. He said, "Moving is a kind of answer. I saw a bull moose yesterday, rooting around. He didn't stay long, just kept walking on those tall, stilted legs. I don't need to know anything else when I see something that perfect. Things happen and change, but then again—a moose can still lift his head on a land blanketed in whiteness, shoot steam from his nostrils, and keep on walking."

Sarah placed her cutting board and an old knife in front of him on the table. Celery, one huge sweet potato, and two carrots shone with wetness. Stew broth rumbled to a boil on the stove. Sarah brushed her hand at Howard like a conductor bringing the final move of a decrescendo into silence. He acquiesced, chopping the vegetables with slow, even strokes.

From the bottom of the hill looking up toward the cabin, someone might have felt warmed by the yellow square of that illuminated kitchen window. But, as it was, nobody was there to see it.

The fish swam on.

acknowledgments

Thank you, first and foremost, to everyone at Gibson House Press. Deb, you heard my narrative voice somewhere in the depths of a global pandemic and believed in the power of the story it told. This book exists because of your enthusiastic support and editorial vision to shepherd it into the world. Mary, your tireless work and marketing expertise carved a path for the novel to reach its readers. Karen, your beautiful design breathes life into the book inside and out.

Thank you to all the organizers of book festivals, author events, creative writing workshops, and writing conferences everywhere. I owe much to the authors who are gracious enough to share their time and wisdom in these spaces. There are too many to name, and all of them are wonderful.

When I began my journey to publication, I had an incredible resource in the Firefly Creative Writing Studio in Toronto. Sincere thanks to Chris, Kelly, and especially Sophia for your restorative well of empathy and craft.

Several people were kind enough to give me encouragement and feedback at various points in the book's evolution. Thank you to everyone who shared an email or phone call with me during the process. Your expertise and encouragement were invaluable: Alyse, Cole, Sequoia, and Eric to name a few.

Thank you to my writing friends who believed in me harder than I could ever believe in myself. You all know who you are, and how eagerly I'm waiting to read your next work. To everyone who has touched my life, all my family and friends, this book has a little piece of you in it.

To all the baristas at all the coffeehouses, you power so many writers you'll never even know about, and we all are grateful for it. To every reader, thank you for being a part of the dream.

Mom and Dad, everything I accomplish springs from the powerful love and sense of wonder you have poured into me since the day I came hungrily into the world. My love for you is endless.

Mike, your pure conviction that this story should live is a huge reason that the book made it anywhere past draft one. I owe you forever, best friend.

Finally, to Scott. Being your wife is the great blessing of my life.

AMY E. CASEY lives and writes in Wisconsin, near the cold freshwater shore of Lake Michigan. From there, she dreams up stories of quiet monsters and wild landscapes. Her short fiction and poetry have been published in *Split Rock Review, Psaltery & Lyre, Club Plum, NonBinary Review, Bramble,* and elsewhere. She does a large portion of her writing on a Smith Corona Classic 12 manual typewriter from 1964. *The Sturgeon's Heart* is her first novel.

GIBSON HOUSE PRESS

connects literary fiction with curious and discerning readers. We publish excellent novels by working musicians and musicians at heart.

GibsonHousePress.com
 GibsonHousePress
 @GibsonPress
 @GHPress

FOR DOWNLOADS OF READING GROUP GUIDES
for Gibson House Press books, visit
GibsonHousePress.com/Reading-Group-Guides